FLAG OF JUDAS

Reversing his mount's direction with a speed and precision which would not have shamed the finest polo player and pony, the brave dropped the head of his weapon forward. Without even trying to shake off the white shirt which had served as a flag, he gave his kill or die cry and signaled his intentions with his heels. Instantly the well-trained horse sprang forward. There was no need for him to think of selecting a victim. He had already decided that only one was suitable and would bring the acclaim deserved by his deed.

The gringo with the face of *el diablo*!

Ole Devil and the Mule Train

J. T. EDSON

A DELL BOOK

Published by
Dell Publishing
a division of
Bantam Doubleday Dell Publishing Group, Inc.
666 Fifth Avenue
New York, New York 10103

The trademark Dell® is registered in the U.S. Patent and Trademark Office.

ISBN: 0-440-21036-4

Printed in the United States of America

Published simultaneously in Canada

June 1992

10 9 8 7 6 5 4 3 2 1

RAD

For William D. "Bo" Randall, Jr., and his son Gary of Orlando, Florida, makers of damned fine knives

1
HOW THE HELL DID THEY LET IT HAPPEN?

There had been death in plenty at the top of the hollow which surrounded Santa Cristóbal Bay, some ten miles north of the Matagorda Peninsula, Texas, on the morning of February 28, 1836. The bodies of many horses and men lay in a mass some fifty or so yards from the rim, their lifeblood thick upon the ground.

A few of the corpses were Mexicans, clad in fancy light green uniforms of the style worn by hussars and other light cavalry regiments in Europe. The remainder were Indians, but not of the kind who might have been expected in East Texas. They were tall and lean for the most part, and their garments were multihued cotton shirts hanging outside trousers which were tucked into the knee-high leggings of moccasins. Weapons of various types were scattered about, discarded by their lifeless owners. There were the officers' swords, the enlisted men's tomahawks, lances, primitive yet effective curved wooden throwing sticks, bows and arrows, but few firearms.

The commanding officer of the Arizona Hopi Activos Regiment, who lay with a large proportion of the three companies which he had sent into the attack, had based his strategy upon the fact that there was always a serious failing of flintlock rifles and pistols in chilly and damp weather conditions.[1] He had stated that the regiment would rely upon cold steel. Shattered open by one of the defender's bullets, his skull was testimony to the fact that he had made a terrible miscalculation.

In spite of all the slaughter they had inflicted that morning, it seemed the victors still had not become sated by fighting and wanted to see more killing.

Gathered in a rough circle around a pair of young men who were facing each other and holding bared knives, it was plain that those responsible for the corpses belonged to two separate parties. They were, in fact, members of the Texas Light Cavalry and the Red River Volunteer Dragoons, both part of the recently organized army of the Republic of Texas.

Like the majority of the other Texians[2] and Chicanos[3] who were fighting to obtain freedom from Mexican domination, the two groups of men who had defeated the attack by a much larger force—the purpose of which was to capture a valuable shipment of arms—belonged to privately raised outfits.

The Texas Light Cavalry showed the greatest uniformity in attire and weapons. Its members wore low-crowned, wide-brimmed black hats of a pattern which had become popular among the Anglo-U.S. colonists, particularly as the oppressive policies of Presidente Antonio López de Santa Anna had caused an increasing antipathy toward everything of Mexican origin. Their fringed buckskin shirts were tucked into fawn riding breeches, which ended in black Hessian

1. Another and even more serious example of the effect of inclement weather conditions on firearms using the flintlock system is given in *Ole Devil at San Jacinto*.
2. Texian: an Anglo-U.S.–born citizen of Mexico, the *i* being dropped from general usage after annexation by the United States of America and the conclusion of the 1846–48 war with Mexico.
3. Chicano: a Mexican-born citizen of Texas.

boots.[4] Each of them had a pistol carried butt forward on a broad, slanting leather loop at the right side of the waist belt, so that it would be accessible to either hand, and had a knife of some kind sheathed on the left. While their garments were stained and untidy, it was from hard usage and long traveling rather than neglect.

However, while the Red River Volunteer Dragoons also sported buckskin shirts, they had retained whatever style of headdress, trousers, footwear, and armament they had had in their possession at the time of enlistment. In most cases, their dirty and disheveled aspect stemmed from a complete uninterest in their personal appearance.

The combatants in the center of the circle were about the same age, in their early twenties. At close to six feet, they were evenly matched in height and weight. From all appearances, there was little between them where skill was concerned. Crouching slightly, with the knife's blade extended in front of the thumb and forefinger of the right hand—a grip permitting a variety of cuts or thrusts—each used his left hand as an aid to his balance as well as to try to distract or grab hold of the other. Moving warily around, they watched for their chances and launched or evaded attacks.

"Go get him, Alvin!" yelled one of the dragoons as the representative of his outfit made a fast stride rearward to avoid a low thrust.

"Keep after him, Stepin!" encouraged one of the cavalrymen, watching the fighter in the fawn breeches press forward to make another attempt at driving home his weapon. "You've got him on the run!"

There were other pieces of advice, some similar and others conflicting, supplied by various members of the crowd. Being so engrossed in watching and exhorting, none of them noticed the two groups of riders who were approaching. The

4. Hessian boots: originally designed for use by light cavalry such as hussars, having legs which extend to just below the knee and with a V-shaped notch at the front.

first, consisting of three young men, was coming at a gallop and was about a quarter of a mile ahead of the second, larger—eleven strong—party.

If the Texas Light Cavalry's contingent around the fight had been aware of the leading trio's presence, particularly that of the man in front, not even their excitement would have prevented them from realizing that they were behaving in a most unsatisfactory and undesirable fashion. They would also have realized that they were likely to have the point brought home to them, aware or otherwise, in no uncertain fashion.

Having seen and heard the commotion, as he and his companions were returning from the successful pursuit of the person who had been responsible for the Arizona Hopi Activos Regiment's attack, Captain Jackson Baines Hardin—commanding officer of Company C, Texas Light Cavalry—acted with his usual promptitude but also showed the kind of forethought and understanding that made him one of the regiment's most successful fighting leaders.

Those same qualities had caused Captain Hardin to be given responsibility for handling his present assignment. It was one upon which the future of Texas might be hinged. So the last thing he wanted was further trouble and difficulties, particularly such as might accrue from a fight between his men and the other group that had been thrown into their company at such an opportune moment.

Since circumstances had caused Captain Hardin to leave Louisiana and would make it impossible for him to return,[5] he had become deeply involved in the Texians' struggle for independence. That was only to have been expected. Other members of the wealthy and influential Hardin, Fog, and Blaze clan had already made their homes in what was at that

5. The circumstances are explained in *Ole Devil and the Caplocks*.

time a territory of the state of Coahuila[6] and had welcomed him to their midst. When it had become obvious that open conflict with Mexico was unavoidable, they had financed, recruited, and equipped the small regiment in which he was now serving.

The Hardin, Fog, and Blaze clan was a stout supporter of the strategy proposed by Major General Samuel Houston, who had been given command of the Republic of Texas's[7] hastily assembled army. They had willingly accepted his decision to withdraw to the east. They had shared his understanding that it would be disastrous to make a stand against the vastly superior numbers of the force that Santa Anna was already marching north to quell their uprising, unless it was at a time and in a place of their own choosing. While retiring, they were to harass the Mexicans with hit-and-run tactics calculated to create as much havoc as possible.

However, Captain Hardin had been taken away from the regiment and was handling an important mission. A consignment of five hundred new percussion-fired caplock rifles and a large supply of ammunition had been donated by sympathizers and had been dispatched by sea from New Orleans. Because of the delicate political situation in the United States of America, where feelings were sharply divided over the rebellion,[8] it had been considered advisable to keep the consignment a secret. So it was landed at Santa Cristóbal

6. Presidente Santa Anna's repeated refusals to make Texas a separate state with full representation in the Mexican government had been a major cause of the rebellion.
7. Although it would not be until March 2, 1836, that a convention at Washington-on-the-Brazos declared Texas a free and independent republic under the Lone Star flag, many Texians had been referring to it in such a manner since the previous year's conflict with the Mexican authorities had ended all hopes of a peaceful settlement.
8. Knowing many prominent Texians believed their only secure future lay in annexation of the republic by the United States of America, the liberal antislavery factions were afraid that doing so would increase the power of the proslavery lobby. The Texians had suggested that in view of the vast area of land which was involved, Texas could be divided into three or four

Bay, instead of being delivered through one of the seaports which were in the Texians' hands. Company C was under orders to collect the consignment and, transporting it by Ewart Brindley's mule train, take it to wherever General Houston and the rest of the army might be.

A band of renegades led by Madeline de Moreau and her husband had learned of the shipment. Before they could be disposed of, in addition to wounding Ewart Brindley and his *cargador*, assistant packmaster, Joe Galton, they had killed the train's bell mare. However, Brindley's granddaughter, Charlotte Martha Jane—who was more usually referred to as Diamond Hitch, shortened to Di, because of her speed and efficiency in throwing[9] such a fastening on a mule's pack —was fully capable of handling the train.

With her husband already dead, Madeline de Moreau's last fling had been to guide the three companies of the Arizona Hopi Activos Regiment—also a volunteer outfit consisting of Mexican officers and Indian enlisted men—to the bay. Having learned that they were coming, Captain Hardin had conceived a most effective defensive plan. The attack had been driven off with heavy losses, ending in the deaths of the woman, all but one of the officers, and many of the Hopis' chiefs and war leaders who were serving as noncoms.

While it had still left them outnumbered by almost two to one, the arrival of Major Ludwig von Löwenbräu and thirty members of the Red River Volunteer Dragoons had given Captain Hardin the means by which he could defeat the larger enemy force. However, there had been a time when the newcomers' presence had appeared to be anything but a blessing.

Having found out about the shipment of arms and ammunition, Colonel Frank Johnson—the founder of the Red River Volunteer Dragoons—had seen how it could be put to

---

separate states. The abolitionists claimed that these would join the others that already supported the continuance of slavery.
9. A mule packer never used the word *tied* but always said he was throwing a diamond hitch on his animal's load.

his private use. Ignoring Houston's strategy and orders to the contrary, he was planning—as he put it—to carry the war to the enemy by invading Mexico along the coast road. Not knowing that Captain Hardin had arranged for Company C to act as an escort for the mule train, he had sent von Löwenbräu to confiscate the consignment. Nor had he given a thought to how the loss might affect the rest of the Republic of Texas's army. He was solely concerned with the loot and acclaim which would accrue from the successful conclusion of his scheme. Being foiled in the attempt, the Prussian had elected to desert Johnson and transfer with his men to the Texas Light Cavalry.

On seeing and realizing what must be causing the commotion at the top of the rim, Captain Hardin began to doubt the wisdom of having agreed to von Löwenbräu's suggestion. He was also furious that such a situation had been allowed to develop and take place in his temporary absence. Not that he could blame von Löwenbräu, who had been knocked unconscious by a Hopi throwing stick and had not yet recovered. In addition, Sergeant Maxime of Company C had been killed by an arrow, and Corporal Anchor wounded in the hand-to-hand fighting. Sergeant Dale had led the party that had followed ready to support himself and his two companions when they had gone after Diamond Hitch Brindley in pursuit of Madeline de Moreau.

However, that had still left all of the dragoons' noncoms and Corporal Smith, who had earned his promotion for the part he had played in preventing the confiscation of the consignment. While none of the former would have attained their ranks in Company C, the latter ought to have been intelligent enough to have seen the trouble brewing and tried to avert it.

"God damn it to hell and back!" the young captain had raged. "How the hell did they let it happen?"

In spite of his anger and desire to bring the potentially explosive situation to an end, Captain Hardin had appreciated the disadvantages of charging up at the head of the party that was with him. Veterans all, disciplined and obedient as they were, the enlisted men, if used to quell the disturbance, would be likely to side with the other members of Company C. Even if they had no such intention, the dragoons would have expected it of them and acted accordingly.

With that in mind, the captain had ordered Sergeant Dale to return at a slower pace and take care of Di, who had lost her horse and was riding double with him. Then, having transferred the girl to the noncom's mount, he had set off at a gallop, accompanied by only two companions. However, he was confident that the pair were adequate for his needs, each having special qualities which made him particularly suited to the task. With their assistance, he hoped to break up the crowd before they got completely out of hand. Even so, he knew it was not going to be easy.

Six feet in height, First Lieutenant Mannen Blaze was dressed in a somewhat better-quality version of the enlisted men's uniform, but with a scarlet silk bandanna tightly rolled and knotted around his throat. He had a .54 caliber Manton[10] caplock pistol and a massive ivory-handled knife of the kind which had already acquired the name bowie in honor of the man credited with the design of the original weapon. Although he was bulky in build and generally conveyed an impression of well-padded, contented lassitude, the men under his command—and others who had been fooled until they had learned the error of their ways—realized that his demeanor was deceptive. For all his size, he was not clumsy. He could move fast when necessary and possessed great strength. Some indication of the former was shown by the way in which he sat his powerful brown gelding, being a light rider for all his weight.

So, while on the surface the burly red-haired young man appeared somnolent to the point of being a dullard, in reality

10. Joseph ("Old Joe") Manton, a gunsmith of London, England, who was an early maker of fine-quality percussion-fired rifles and pistols.

he was a smart and capable officer. It had been his quick grasp of the situation and his adroit manipulations which, in Captain Hardin's absence, had bluffed von Löwenbräu out of attempting to gain possession of the consignment.

On the face of it, the second of the young captain's assistants seemed to warrant even less confidence than Mannen Blaze. He was not quite five feet six inches in height, but with a sturdy physique, and his almond-eyed and cheerful features were those of a native of the Orient. Bareheaded, he had closely cropped black hair. His garments were a loose-fitting and wide-sleeved black shirt hanging outside trousers of the same material which were tucked into matching Hessian boots.

Apart from his footwear and the lack of a pigtail, the man could have been a Chinese coolie who might be found in any of the United States' major seaports. However, one rarely saw a coolie carrying weapons, and he appeared to be well armed, if in a somewhat primitive fashion. A pair of long-handled, slightly curved swords with small, circular guards balanced each other—the shorter at the right—in lacquered bamboo sheaths attached by slings to his leather waist belt. In addition, he grasped a bow at least six feet in length in his left fist, and there was a quiver suspended across his back so that its arrows would be readily accessible to his right hand.[11]

As with Mannen Blaze, Tommy Okasi's looks were deceptive. There was little contact between his homeland and the Western Hemisphere, nor would there be until after the visits in 1853–54 of a flotilla of warships commanded by Commodore Perry, United States Navy, so few people knew that

11. Traditionally a Japanese samurai warrior's daisho—a matched pair of swords comprised of the tachi, with a thirty-inch blade, and the wakizashi, about half the former's blade length—were carried thrust through the girdle. As Tommy Okasi had had to spend long hours on horseback since arriving in the United States and accompanying Ole Devil Hardin to Texas, he had found it more convenient to equip the sheaths with slings and carry them on either side of his belt.

he had originated from the group of islands known collectively as Japan. They believed him to be Chinese. He was reticent about his reasons for leaving, and because he was exceptionally capable in his nation's highly effective martial arts, for the most part his privacy was respected. Those who tried to invade it never repeated the attempt.

For all his undoubted skill as a warrior, the little Oriental was content to act as Captain Hardin's valet. He had always proved to be a cheerful, loyal, courageous, and dependable companion, being willing to take any risk which became necessary. These admirable traits had been displayed many times, even before accompanying his employer to Texas and taking an active part in the present assignment.

Matching Mannen Blaze in height, attire—with the exception that his tightly rolled silk bandanna was a riot of clashing, multihued colors—age (in the mid-twenties), and armament, Jackson Baines Hardin was slender without being skinny or puny. Even while riding at a good speed across uneven terrain, he sat his linebacked dun gelding with a ramrod-straight erectness. Although travel-stained and somewhat disheveled, his clothing showed signs that he had endeavored to keep it as clean as possible.

The most remarkable feature about the young commanding officer of Company C, especially at such a moment, was his face. Combed back and exposed by having his hat hanging on his shoulders by its *barbiquejo,* chin strap, his coal black hair formed what looked like small, curved horns above his temples. Taken with eyebrows like inverted *V*'s, lean cheeks, an aquiline nose, a neatly trimmed mustache— he had shaved that morning—and a short, sharply pointed chin beard, they created a satanic aspect which, in part, had produced his nickname, Ole Devil.[12]

Bringing the dun to a rump-sliding halt about thirty feet from the still-unsuspecting and rowdy mob, the young cap-

12. Another cause of Jackson Baines Hardin's nickname was his well-deserved reputation for being a "lil ole devil for a fight."

tain quit its low-horned, double-girthed[13] saddle and released its split-ended reins. Doing so ensured that the animal would not stray. It had been trained to stand still when ground hitched by the dangling strands of leather and would move only under the direst of provocation.

Without even so much as a glance at his two companions, knowing that he could rely implicitly upon their judgment, Ole Devil Hardin strode forward with sharp and angry strides. Since taking on the mission, he had had to deal ruthlessly with several situations and was willing to do so on this occasion. Nor would the fact that his own men were involved prevent him from taking whatever steps he considered necessary. For all that, he knew a single mistake on his part could blow the whole affair up into something which neither he nor anybody else could handle.

13. Because of its Mexican derivation, from the word *cincha,* Texians tended to use the term *girth* rather than *cinch.*

2

I'LL MAKE YOU SORRY YOU
WERE BORN!

Selecting a portion of the onlookers comprised of his own men, from whom he felt he could produce the most desired effect, Ole Devil Hardin headed straight for it. He heard footsteps on either side and a few paces to his rear. So he knew that Mannen Blaze and Tommy Okasi were following in the same rough arrowhead formation in which they had been riding. Although he did not see that the little Oriental no longer carried the bow and, by tugging at the quick-release knot of the carrying strap, had removed and left both it and the quiver near the horses, he would have felt no qualms if he had. Even without his daisho, Tommy's ability in the little publicized—outside his homeland—unarmed combat techniques of jujitsu and karate made him more than a match for most bigger, heavier, and stronger assailants.

Two of the spectators, who were clad in fawn riding breeches, felt themselves being pushed roughly from the rear by somebody who clearly wanted to pass between them. Turning, bristling with indignation and ready to take reprisals, they found themselves confronted by a figure whose features were meaner than—and very much like the pictures they had seen of—Old Nick as he was stoking up the fiery furnaces to roast another bunch of miserable sinners. Although they realized that the owner of the face was considerably more earthly and mundane, the effect was pretty near the same.

In fact, the pair were aware that somebody was sure as hell going to find themselves pretty close to being roasted in the *very* near future. Assuming expressions which they hoped showed indifference, trying to appear innocent, they lost all their hostility. Once their commanding officer had stalked by, they began to edge backward with the intention of disassociating themselves from a situation that they felt sure would *not* meet with his approval.

Glancing at Tommy, Mannen diverged from the line being taken by his cousin and passed around the circle to the right. Without needing advice, the little Oriental hurried in the opposite direction until he reached the dividing line between the dragoons and the left flank of Company C. It was, he concluded as he entered the gap, fortunate that he had demonstrated his skill at *lai jitsu,* the fast withdrawal of the tachi, during the final stages of the fight and also how deadly effective such a weapon could be in his trained hands. It would be a fine inducement toward compliance with orders and a warning that any attempt to extend the hostilities would be extremely dangerous.

For his part, the burly red-haired lieutenant seemed to be almost on the point of falling asleep as he elbowed his way through the other narrow space separating the two factions. A few from each group turned with angry protests on their lips, but none of them continued with their complaints. All of them were aware of his true potential and were not fooled by his languid exterior. However, before he could emerge beyond them, he saw something which demanded his immediate attention.

On arriving at the forefront of the circle, Ole Devil took in the situation with a swift look. He found some slight relief in noticing that, as yet, there was no mingling between the members of the two companies. That made things just a little more stable, provided the dragoons did not attempt to take their representative's part. He was counting upon his companions and the speed with which he must now act to prevent trouble.

Although Ole Devil had never heard of psychology, he realized that the more spectacularly he dealt with the situation, the greater its effect would be upon the onlookers. In this he would be aided by his knowledge of savate, the foot and fist fighting practiced by French Creoles in Louisiana. Furthermore, while he did not possess the skill which would be acquired by another—as yet unborn—member of the Hardin, Fog, and Blaze clan,[1] Tommy had taught him several useful jujitsu and karate tricks. Utilizing his combined lessons in the art of self-defense, he felt he could achieve his purpose—particularly as, seeming to wish to help him, the combatants were close together. Each having grasped the other's right wrist with the left hand, they were straining to gain the advantage.

Thrusting himself forward without waiting for Mannen or Tommy to emerge from the crowd, the captain darted toward the two young men. He bounded into the air, rotating his body until it was parallel to the ground. Unfortunately, an instant before he reached them, they decided their position was at a deadlock and, as if by mutual consent—or realizing another factor was entering the game—shoved each other away. So they were just too far separated to receive the full impact of the collision.

While Ole Devil still struck the fighters and sent them staggering, his attack lacked the force to incapacitate them. They went reeling at angles away from each other, but without losing their holds on the knives. Having been hit slightly the harder, the cavalryman sprawled to his hands and knees.

1. The member in question was Dustine Edward Marsden ("Dusty") Fog, whose history and fighting abilities are recorded in the author's Civil War and Floating Outfit series of biographies.

Blundering onward for a few more paces, the dragoon contrived to remain erect. Alighting on his feet, Ole Devil glared from one to the other, knowing the affair was not yet over.

Muttering an oath, one of von Löwenbräu's men standing at the edge of their group reached for the pistol which was thrust into his belt. A friend of the knife fighter, he felt it was incumbent upon him to register a protest over such an unfair intervention by a man clad in the fashion of the opposition. Before he could do so or identify the interloper—not that he would have been influenced toward wisdom by the discovery —he experienced a sensation such as might have resulted if he had allowed his right shoulder to come between the jaws of an exceptionally powerful bear trap.

"Now you just leave that be and stay out of it, *please*," requested a drawling and lethargic voice, which somehow sounded as chilling as if it had been snarled ferociously. The last word of the sentence was accompanied by an even greater crushing pressure on the shoulder. "Because, if you don't, I'll make you sorry you were born!"

Numbed with agony, the dragoon glanced behind him. Maybe some folks would have regarded the bland features which met his gaze as belonging to a dull-witted simpleton, but he was not among their number. Recognizing his captor, he would have obeyed even if the excruciating torment being inflicted by the largest thumb and fingers he had ever seen were leaving him with a second choice.

Noticing that several members of both factions appeared to be contemplating hostile action, either for or against his employer, Tommy Okasi sprang to confront them. In a flickering blur of motion, which would be matched only by top-grade gunfighters—with much shorter weapons—using techniques developed from the late 1860s to the present day, he whipped the thirty-inch-long razor-sharp blade of the tachi from its sheath.

"Ancient Nipponese saying, which I've just made up," the little Oriental announced, in sibilant tones and using very good English, as he brandished the sword in both hands.

"Man who pokes his nose into thing which must be stopped for good of all could end up walking on his knees, having lost all that is below them."

As in Mannen's case, there were those alive who might have regarded such behavior, coming as it did from so short a person in the presence of many larger men, as being fool-hardy to say the least.

However, several of Tommy's audience had seen and told the majority of the rest how he had practically decapitated— although that was not the term used by those who described the incident—a large Hopi brave who was trying to gut him with a war lance. Then, even before the corpse had struck the ground, he had pivoted through a good ninety degrees to fell a second warrior harboring similar intentions toward him.

So the listeners did not regard the little Oriental's politely phrased words as other than a serious warning of the action he was willing to take if necessary.

Without being aware of the way in which his companions were supporting and protecting him, although neither of their tactics would have been a surprise, Ole Devil prepared to bring the fight to an end.

Being on his feet, the dragoon posed the greater and more pressing threat.

Unfortunately the problem was not so simple as there was the future to consider.

The man's companions would be resentful of anything which they regarded as a show of favoritism on the young captain's part.

Accepting what could be the only solution, Ole Devil started to put it into effect. His conscience was soothed by knowing the nature of his company's representative in the fight. Stepin had always shown considerable reluctance to accept discipline, despite being loyal to his outfit and proud to be serving in it, and in the past his behavior on a number of occasions had come very close to warranting punishment.

Leaping forward, as the cursing cavalryman began to rise,

Ole Devil swung up his right leg. Well versed in savate, he sent the toe of his boot with carefully calculated force under Stepin's chin. Back snapped the head of the recipient of the attack. Lifted upward a few inches, he released his knife's hilt and collapsed limply to the ground. It was obvious that he would not be taking any further interest in the proceedings for a few minutes at least.

However, the dragoon was already rushing to the attack. He hoped that he would take his second assailant by surprise and repay the unprovoked assault upon him.

The hope did not materialize!

Instead of waiting for his assailant to reach him, Ole Devil glided forward on what appeared to be a converging course.

Intending to drive his knife "up to the 'Green River' "[2] into the intruder's belly, the dragoon became aware of how his would-be victim looked. Studying the savage, Mephistophelian features, he could not help glancing down. It came almost as a surprise and relief to discover that the other did not have cloven hooves or a forked tail but was clad in the attire of the Texas Light Cavalry.

The understanding came a trifle too late.

Swinging to face his attacker, Ole Devil watched the knife as it was driven toward his midsection. At the last moment he rotated his torso clear by swinging his left foot in a circular motion to his rear. Simultaneously he raised both hands to shoulder height, palm downward. Bringing them together, he sent them to clamp hold of Wilkie's right wrist and force it downward away from him. Taking his weight on the right foot, the captain bent his left knee until its thigh was parallel to the ground. Still guiding the point of the knife in a harmless direction, he pulled with his hands and snapped around

2. First produced on the Green River, at Greenfield, Massachusetts, in 1834, a very popular type of knife had the following inscription on its blade just below the hilt: "J. Russell & Co./Green River Works." Any knife thrust into an enemy "up to the 'Green River' "—whether it bore the inscription or not—would be fatal.

the raised limb so that the knee took his attacker in the pit of the stomach. Then, with a surging heave, he flung the winded, folded-over, and helpless young man with a flipping motion. Turning a half somersault, Wilkie alighted supine and with a bone-jarring thud which drove all the air from his lungs and stunned him. Like Stepin, he was no longer in any condition to resume hostilities.

Having ended the main source of dissension, Ole Devil wasted no time in setting about removing the rest. Glancing quickly at the two recumbent soldiers, to ensure that neither was going to make further trouble, he turned and raked the crowd with his cold black eyes. Noticing in passing that Mannen and Tommy had fully justified his confidence in them, he sought for the means to put into operation his father's advice upon how to handle such a situation.

"When you're dealing with an unruly mob, particularly if the men in it are subject to some form of discipline," Captain Jeremiah Hardin, master of the trading ship *Star of the Southland*—which had brought Tommy Okasi to the United States—had counseled, "pick out one of them and make it look like you hold *him* responsible for what's happening."

Few of the dragoons and none of Company C would meet the grim-faced young captain's angry scrutiny. Fortunately the one he had selected to be his target did so.

"All right, *Sergeant* Otis!" Ole Devil growled, staring at the burly man who was standing in the center of the dragoons. "How did *you* let it start?"

"M-me?" the designated soldier began, becoming aware that the men on either side of him had begun to edge away furtively.

"Hell, Cap'n, all young—" commenced a member of Company C, but the words trailed away as his superior's satanic face turned in his direction.

"Just how the hell long have *you* been Sergeant Otis?" Ole Devil demanded, with cold and savage fury which caused its recipient to back off and put aside all notions of making an explanation. On returning his gaze to its original subject, he

found to his satisfaction that the noncom was no longer eye-
ing him defiantly but was looking at the ground as if finding
it of absorbing interest. "Well, *Sergeant*?"

"It was all the fault of them damned fly-slicers[3] of yourn,"
Otis mumbled, jerking an indignant thumb toward the cavalryman. "They reckoned—"

"I don't know how it is in the Red River Volunteer
Dragoons, *Sergeant*!" Ole Devil interrupted, after having si-
lenced his men's muttered protests with a glare. "But in *my*
regiment, which *you're* figuring on joining, you address an
officer by his rank or call him sir."

"Well—sir," Otis went on, the honorific popping like a
cork from a bottle as the captain's right foot tapped on the
ground in warning, "it was— They reckoned's how us
dragoons didn't do our share of the fighting."

"Hell, Cap'n!" yelled one of Stepin's boon companions.
"They took their time—"

"Mr. Blaze!" Ole Devil thundered, above the growls of
objection from the dragoons. "Put that man to the hardest,
dirtiest job you can find—and look for some more that need
doing!"

"Yo!" Mannen boomed, giving the traditional cavalry ac-
knowledgment. Having anticipated how his cousin would re-
act to the interference, he was already ambling in the required direction with what could only be described as
leisurely alacrity. "Get the hell into the hollow and ask Joe
Galton to give you something to start digging with."

Satisfied that his second-in-command could deal with that
aspect of the situation, Ole Devil returned his attention to
the discomforted sergeant.

"Hell—sir!" Otis spit out. "We done our fair share, and
we was on top here in them rifle pits right from the start.

3. Fly-slicers: derogatory name for members of the cavalry as opposed to
dragoons, who, although mounted for the purpose of traveling, usually
fought on foot.

And we got out of 'em's quick's we could when you yelled for us to charge. So why—"

"I wasn't asking for a debate upon our action against the enemy, Sergeant," Ole Devil pointed out coldly. "My question to you, the only one to which I require an answer, is how did *you* let the fight start."

Nothing about the young captain's Mephistophelian features suggested that he, too, had noticed that the dragoons had been slow in quitting the rifle pits when he had given the order to engage the Hopis at close quarters. He could see what had happened. Always arrogant and hotheaded, Stepin must have commented upon their dilatoriness. Being of a similar disposition, Wilkie had taken offense. However, the last thing Ole Devil wanted was to have the matter retained as part of the conversation.

"Hell, Cap'n," Otis began, "we was all just standing around—"

"Why?" Ole Devil asked.

"Huh?" the sergeant grunted, showing puzzlement.

"Why were you all just *standing* around?" Ole Devil elaborated, wondering where Corporal Smith had been and why he had not organized some kind of work to keep at least Company C occupied.

"You'd all gone after the Brindley gal," Otis explained. "Von Low—the major was unconscious, and that Rassendyll feller'd got an arrow in his shoul—"

"I don't need a casualty list, Sergeant," the captain interrupted, and realizing that he had not seen any of the wounded as he was returning, deduced that his missing corporal had organized their removal into the hollow so that they could receive medical attention. "What you're trying to say is that nobody had given *you* any orders and *you* didn't have enough damned sense to put the men to work without them."

"Well— That is—" Otis mumbled, hanging his head and shuffling his feet.

"You're not under *my* command," Ole Devil stated, and

although he did not say "Thank God," the words were there. "And I'll leave it to Major von Löwenbräu as to what action he takes against you. However, in his absence, *Sergeant*, I'd be obliged if you would put yourself and your men at Mr. Blaze's disposal so that *he* can tell you what needs to be done."

"Yes, sir," Otis responded, throwing angry glares at his companions rather than toward the man who was delivering the tongue-lashing.

"You men of Company C get started throwing the Mexicans' and Indians' bodies into the sea," Mannen commanded, having heard what was being said. Shrewdly he realized that his cousin was expecting him to act without waiting for instructions so as to emphasize the point made to Otis. "Put *your* dragoons to helping them, Sergeant. I'll leave you in charge of the burial detail. Take those two yacks lying there, as soon as they can stand. Have the one I sent to fetch shovels and a man from your company. I'd say the one rubbing his shoulder, but that's up to *you*. Then get graves for our dead dug up here."

"Yes, sir," Otis answered, showing as little hesitation in giving the honorific to the redhead as he had to the captain.

Not for the first time, Ole Devil blessed his good fortune in having such an excellent second-in-command. Mannen had done exactly the right thing by putting their own men to work before dealing with the dragoons and in letting Otis be responsible for the way in which the latter carried it out. The division of labor and the choice of personnel for the gravedigging detail had also been as expertly handled as the captain could have wished it. While he had no idea why the dragoon was rubbing his shoulder, he felt sure that his cousin had had a sound reason for making that selection. Certainly the behavior of the other three had been bad enough to warrant the punishment. What was more, putting Otis in direct charge of them was an equally shrewd move. Smarting with humiliation, he was likely to pay greater attention than he had done previously in performing his duties and keeping them hard at work.

Despite his satisfaction with Mannen's handling of the situation and his belief that he could rely upon Otis, Ole Devil decided to stay on the rim. By reminding them that retribution was close at hand, his presence would tend to act as a calming influence on any recalcitrant spirits.

"I've let Di take my horse and ride down to see Doc Kimberley so that she can tell her grandpappy she's all right, sir," Sergeant Dale reported, striding up at that moment. Being just as good a judge of the situation as Mannen, he delivered a very smart salute. "Looks like you've quieted them down for a spell."

"Yes," Ole Devil agreed. "For a spell."

"You reckon they'll be loco enough to get to fussing again, Cap'n?" Dale inquired.

"There's always that danger once it's been started," Ole Devil warned. "So we'll have to—"

At that moment Corporal Smith appeared from the hollow. A big blond-haired man in his early thirties, he moved with an erect carriage which suggested that he had had military training. Glancing around, he seemed both pleased and relieved with what he saw. Then he strode forward but halted a short distance away from where his three superiors were standing.

"Yes, Corporal?" Ole Devil asked.

"I'm sorry I didn't get here before, sir," Smith answered, after he had advanced and saluted. "By the time I'd heard the ruckus and started up, you must have come back and stopped it."

"That's all right, I don't blame you," Ole Devil replied. "How're things down in the hollow?"

"Major von Löwenbräu's recovered but won't be in any shape to ride today, Doc Kimberley says, sir," Smith replied. "Mr. Rassendyll's as well as can be expected, and none of the others are too serious. Two of them'll need to ride a travois and the Tejas'll be making one apiece for them as soon as they can."

"*Bueno*," Ole Devil said in praise, feeling sure that the arrangements had been made at Smith's instigation and liking the corporal all the more for not having mentioned the fact. "Take rank of sergeant in Sergeant Maxime's place."

"*Gracias*, Captain," Smith said, showing his pleasure at the promotion. "Thing is, though, sir, Doc asked me to tell you he'd like to get Ewart Brindley and the other two to Washington-on-the-Brazos as quickly as possible, so he can get them attended to properly. Like he says, he hasn't the gear to do it himself."

"It'll be noon at least before we'll be ready to pull out," Mannen put in thoughtfully.

"If then," Ole Devil went on, then looked to where Stepin and Wilkie were on their feet and scowling at each other. "Mr. Blaze, give Sergeant Otis my compliments and tell him that I intend to hold the burial services on our dead in ninety minutes so the graves had better be ready by then."

"Yo!" the redhead answered, and turned to deliver the message without waiting to find out why there was such urgency.

3
VON LÖWENBRÄU'S UP TO SOMETHING

Prays Loudly, Sometimes, the Tejas Indian mule packer, had been in old Ewart Brindley's employment for close to ten years. During that time he had become competent in his work and could be trusted to carry out every part of it without needing to be supervised. So, but for one *very* important detail, he might have taken grave exception to having somebody—particularly a person who knew little or nothing about the finer points of his specialized trade—standing close by watching him. What was more, in spite of the low regard which many Texians and Chicanos had for members of his nation as warriors, he was tough enough and possessed sufficient weapons savvy to back up any protests that he cared to make.

However, bearing in mind various recent events, Prays Loudly, Sometimes felt that the man in question had earned the right to carry out an unchallenged scrutiny. In fact, guessing the reason for it, he even experienced a sense of pride that he had been selected from all his fellow workers to be watched. It was most flattering that a war chief of *Diablo Viejo*'s well-deserved reputation should consider that he, of all the mule train's experienced and accomplished packers, was the one most worthy of being watched and learned from.

As the late February weather tended to be chilly and damp, particularly so soon after dawn, Ole Devil Hardin had his black cloak coat—its front, open and sleeves empty—draped across his squared shoulders. However, despite the inclement conditions, his black hat was still hanging on his back.

Possessing an active and inquiring mind, Ole Devil invariably took an interest in anything he believed might one day be of service to him. He had neither the desire nor the intention of going into active business competition with Ewart Brindley, but he did consider that the time might come when having a knowledge of mule packing could prove advantageous. So, having made all his own arrangements, he was grabbing the opportunity to watch some of the preparations which were being carried out for the most important aspect of the return journey. He was hoping that he would not be interrupted before he had satisfied his curiosity, as had happened the day before, while they had been getting ready to leave Santa Cristóbal Bay.

Nothing had happened so far, and Ole Devil was waiting with eager anticipation to see what would be done. As on the previous morning, before the arrival of the Arizona Hopi Activos Regiment had ended it, the seemingly confused activity taking place before him was nothing of the kind. It was being carried out by the pick of the cream of the mule-packing profession. So the men concerned went about their work with a speed and purpose which told of years of practical experience.

Although Major General Samuel Houston had requested that Brindley sent the majority of his stock to Washington-on-the-Brazos, to help with the evacuation of what was regarded as the Republic of Texas's capital city[1] and more important, to lessen the chance of their falling into the hands of the enemy, he had retained the best of his men and mules to collect and deliver the consignment.

The train consisted of fifty pack and fourteen riding mules plus the indispensable bell mare. From Ole Devil's examination of the pack animals, he could tell that all were of excellent quality and had been specially selected—in fact, were bred—for their respective duties.

Each of the pack mules was just over fourteen hands in height,[2] with a well-muscled back that was straight or had a slight roach,[3] from the withers to the croup, being broad and level at the top, but having only sufficient length for it to carry its burden without injury to the point of the hip. Wide-chested, with a good breadth at the shoulders, it had the well-developed and powerful quarters so vitally important when traversing hilly terrain while fully loaded. Shortish, clean, and straight at the front, although some tended to be a trifle cow-hocked at the rear[4]—which was no disadvantage as the limbs were free from disease—the legs appeared to be slender when compared with those of a horse. The pack mules were between six and eighteen years of age, fully trained and in the peak of physical condition.

Standing at least a hand taller, longer backed, and with a somewhat lower shoulder to give a better reach when walking, the packers' riding mules were equally well-conditioned animals.

1. The capital was transferred to Austin—named in honor of Stephen Fuller Austin, 1793–1836, one of the first of the Anglo-U.S. colonizers—after the Texians had won their independence.
2. Measured at the withers, the highest part of the back between the shoulder blades, a "hand" being equivalent to four inches.
3. Roach-backed: slightly arched.
4. Cow-hocked: where the legs are curved inward at the hocks—the joints which correspond with the human ankle—so that they are closer together at the pasterns—the part of the leg between hock and hoof—and the stifles, the upper joints of the limbs.

Every packer was in charge of five mules, not counting his personal mount. The cook and Joe Galton, who acted as farrier as well as *cargador,* had an animal apiece assigned to them to carry their respective equipment. On the trail, working with a portable outfit and a selection of ready-made shoes, the farrier had to ensure that the stock were kept well shod at all times. The cook's implements—a sheet iron stove, several camp kettles packed one inside another, a Dutch oven, a coffee mill, a bread pan, a couple of skillets, butcher's knives, and a sharpening steel—were transported in two mess boxes of a suitable size and shape to be attached to a packsaddle.

When deciding to watch one of the packers in action, Ole Devil had asked Diamond Hitch Brindley—who, because of her grandfather's indisposition, was in the position of packmaster—whom she would suggest. Having been directed to Prays Loudly, Sometimes, he had wondered how the brave would regard being under observation. From what the captain could see, he concluded that the other was pleased to have been selected.

Highly skilled at his duties, Prays Loudly, Sometimes was working fast and making the task seem a lot easier than it really was. Taking one of the ready-made cloth blindfolds which were fastened around his arms, he used it to cover the mule's eyes. Doing so ensured that the animal would stand still through the saddling and attaching of its load. It would also be reapplied if there should be any need to adjust the rig and burden during the day's travel. Like most of its kind, while well trained and experienced in its work, the mule was inclined to be highly strung and quick-tempered. Any sudden, unexpected sound or movement could cause it to shy and might end with it kicking and plunging in a dangerous fashion if it was able to see what it was doing; when its eyes were covered, it was inclined to be more passive.

Having taken the precaution, the packer set the sheepskin pad marked with the mule's number—the cook's and farrier's animals were identified by the letters *C* and *F*—and known as a *corona* in position on its back. Next, he took the folded blanket which had formed part of his bedding the previous night and laid it carefully upon the *corona*. This was followed by the *aparejo* type of packsaddle. Specifically designed for the transporting of heavy or awkwardly shaped loads which could not be carried on a conventional packsaddle, it consisted of a pad about twenty-eight inches wide by thirty-six inches long and stuffed with dry, coarse grass to a thickness of three inches. Attached to it were a wide girth and an exceptionally broad—twelve inches in this case—breeching strap which fitted under the animal's tail like a crupper. Adjusted to the appropriate length for that particular beast, being laced to the *aparejo* and padded where it came into contact with the tail, the latter was intended to prevent the load from slipping forward over its wearer's shoulders when going downhill. So important were the correct fit and positioning of the *aparejo* that the line of the mule's back was marked by stitching exactly along its center.

With the breeching in place and the girth drawn tight, Prays Loudly, Sometimes affixed the *sobrejalma*[5] on the *aparejo* and coupled them together with the thongs at the ends of the latter's center line. Made of sturdy tarpaulin, cut to cover the *aparejo* exactly and completely, the *sobrejalma* was faced at the sides and ends with leather. The ends were protected from wrinkling or gathering by having twenty-inch-long sticks—known as shoes—held in place by leather caps, across the bottoms.

Finally, all was tied together with a strong bellyband and a latigo strap. All that remained for Prays Loudly, Sometimes to do was to have the load—two sets of twelve caplock rifles and their bayonets, which had been taken from their shipping boxes and, on being brought ashore wrapped in sailcloth supplied by the vessel that had delivered them—placed upon the assembly. These would then be wrapped in a pack

5. Mule packers in the United States Army called the *sobrejalma* a "hammercloth."

cover and lashed by having a forty- to fifty-foot length of rope throwed around, drawn tight each time, and lashed in the diamond hitch fastening from which the girl had received her nickname.

But once again it seemed that fate was about to decree against Ole Devil's seeing the final preparations of a packer.

Leaving her place by the dead embers of the previous night's fire—it had been put out before daybreak to prevent smoke from rising and attracting unwanted attention—Diamond Hitch Brindley was strolling toward the young captain in what some people might have considered a casual fashion. Having come to know her very well during the time that they had been acquainted, he knew differently. Unless he missed his guess, she was approaching him on a matter of some importance.

About five feet seven inches in height and in her late teens, Di was possessed of a shapely body which was blossoming into full womanhood, a fact the snug fit of her buckskin shirt and trousers, under an open black wolfskin jacket, did little to conceal. She had rawhide moccasins on her feet. There was a pistol thrust through the right side of her waist belt, and a knife hung in an Indian sheath at its left. Somehow, neither they nor the powder horn and bullet bag swinging from her left shoulder seemed incongruous in spite of her obvious femininity. Fairly short and curly red hair framed a pretty freckled face. Nor did having a swollen top lip, a blackened right eye, and a piece of adhesive bandage attached to the lobe of her left ear—gained in the course of two fights, the first barehanded and the second using firearms, against Madeline de Moreau—detract from its charm. Normally her features showed a merry zest for life and a quick, although not bad, temper. Now they held a sober, worried, and annoyed expression.

"What's up, Di?" Ole Devil inquired.

"That high-toned 'n' fancy von Löwenbräu jasper's got all his fellers together," the girl answered, throwing a malevolent glare toward the man she had mentioned. "And was I asked—which I don't expect to be—I wouldn't count on it being just to tell 'em how his lil pumpkin head's still hurting."

Glancing in the direction indicated by the girl, Ole Devil stiffened slightly. He had been so engrossed in watching the packer's preparations that he had paid no attention to anything else that was happening. So he had failed to notice that Major Ludwig von Löwenbräu had gathered the men of the Red River Volunteer Dragoons some distance away and was talking to them. Remembering the decision he had reached and implemented the previous afternoon, the captain wondered if the girl had cause for her alarm.

Matching Ole Devil in height, von Löwenbräu was a few years older and slightly heavier in build. Although there was still a bandage around his close-cropped blond head, he appeared to have thrown off the effects of the injury he had sustained during the fighting. He had been fortunate in that the Hopi's throwing stick had only caught him a glancing blow and stunned him. A direct hit from it would have been fatal.

Despite being attired after the fashion of a successful Mississippi riverboat gambler, except that his footwear was more suited to riding than walking a deck and that he had a saber hanging from the slings of a well-polished waist belt, von Löwenbräu had an even more militaristic bearing than the young captain. Nor was his conception of discipline tempered by the other's sense of humor. He was handsome in a harsh, Teutonic way, with his mustache's tips waxed to sharp points. He also sported the small dueling scars on his cheeks which some students—particularly those who had attended Heidelberg's university—allowed themselves to be marked by as a sign of belonging to a certain class of society.

He had been an officer in his country's army before some unspecified trouble had caused him—like Ole Devil—to have "gone to Texas."[6] Although he had been two grades lower in rank than that to which he now laid claim, he was trained after the fashion of his race. Competent in military matters, skilled in the use of weapons, authoritative, if unimaginative, where formal tactics were concerned, his kind were men to be feared, obeyed, but were rarely liked by the soldiers under their command.

That had certainly been the case with von Löwenbräu. He had soon found that his Prussian-inspired notions of what soldiering should be had availed him little when tried upon the kind of men who were enlisting in the Red River Volunteer Dragoons. It said much for his prowess as a tough and ruthless hardcase that he had attained the rank of major. In fact, that had been one of his arguments when he had offered to transfer his services from Colonel Frank Johnson to the Texas Light Cavalry. To have joined his superior under the stigma of having failed to confiscate the consignment would have given his rivals the lever they needed to bring about his demotion.

Although the Prussian had appeared sincere enough when making the proposal, Ole Devil had soon had cause for misgivings. While he had been making his arrangements for meeting yesterday's attack, von Löwenbräu had acted in a manner which might have been constructed as trying to undermine the captain's authority over the dragoons. Or he could have been—as he had claimed after he had recovered and was congratulating Ole Devil on the successful outcome —merely concerned for the welfare of the men under his command who had been placed in the forefront of the fight-

6. "Gone to Texas": at odds with the law, usually in the United States of America. Many fugitives from justice and wanted men had entered Texas during the colonization period—which had commenced in the early 1820s —and continued to do so until annexation on February 16, 1846. Until the latter became a fact, they had known there was little danger of being arrested and extradited by the local authorities. In fact, like Kenya from the 1920s until the outbreak of World War II, Texas had gained a reputation for being "a place in the sun for shady people."

ing. The declaration had been made in a loud voice, with
most of his men close enough to hear it. For all that, nothing
in his subsequent behavior had suggested he might be contemplating a further attempt to carry out the assignment
which had brought him to Santa Cristóbal Bay.

So, on the face of it, Ole Devil had only slight reasons for
being suspicious. He had left von Löwenbräu in command of
the dragoons, having no authority to do otherwise. In return,
the Prussian had placed himself under Ole Devil's orders.
Knowing that the captain wanted to set off without delay, he
could be ensuring his men were ready. Yet there was something furtive in the way they were acting. Formed into three
ragged ranks, they were displaying considerable interest in
whatever it was their superior was telling them.

Judging from the surreptitious glances being thrown in his
direction, Ole Devil concluded that he could be the topic
under discussion. If so, the situation might require delicate
handling. There was nothing to be gained by allowing von
Löwenbräu to guess that he was arousing suspicions.

"Perhaps he's pointing out what a fine, upstanding figure
of a man I am," Ole Devil suggested, turning his gaze to the
girl, "and how they should take me as an example and
smarten themselves up so they'll be a credit to us when we
take them to join the Texas Light Cavalry."

"Oh, sure!" Di snorted derisively. "And if my grandmammy Brindley's stood up, 'stead of squatting, when she
was having a pee, it'd've been her 'n' not Grandpappy Ewart's took lead back there."

"I didn't know your grandmother was with us," Ole Devil
remarked, and gave the impression that he was going to resume watching Prays Loudly, Sometimes.

"God damn it, Fancy Pants!" the girl began, employing a
name for him which she had not used since early in their
acquaintance. "That son of a bitch's up—"

"Pull your horns in, *Miss Charlotte*!" Ole Devil interrupted, his tone causing Di to stop as she was on the point of

gesturing toward the subject of their conversation and bringing her full attention back to him.

"What the—" the girl spluttered.

"I don't claim to be *real* smart like you," Ole Devil put in, with as much calm as Di was displaying indignation. "So I can't see what benefit—if any—there'd be in rushing over and saying, 'Excuse me, Major von Löwenbräu, sir, we haven't noticed that you might be up to some shenanigans, but if you are, perhaps you'd be good enough to let us in on them.' "

Finding that he was no longer the center of attraction, the Tejas packer was watching and listening. Even though he spoke only a little English, he was aware that Di took very strenuous exception to being addressed by any of her Christian names. That *Diablo Viejo* could do so in such a manner, indeed employ the one she hated most, without her landing her fist in his mouth was, in the opinion of Prays Loudly, Sometimes, further evidence of his capability.

"Ancient Nipponese saying—" said Tommy Okasi's polite voice from behind the girl.

"Which you've just made up," Di groaned, her attitude changing so that she directed a look of mock exasperation at the speaker. "That's *all* I son of a bitching need right now."

To give Di her due, despite her quick temper, she was always willing to listen to sound advice when it was given by someone for whom she had respect. The young Texian and the little Oriental rated highly in her estimation. Having already seen that the former was making good sense and did not take the situation as lightly as his first comment suggested, she welcomed the latter's intervention as it allowed her to yield without openly surrendering.

"Woman's place is in home or geisha teahouse," Tommy continued, "not trying to tell men what to do."

"It's a pity your mammy ever went home," Di answered.

"She *never* left it," the little Oriental countered blandly. "Nipponese woman—"

"What do *you* reckon von Löwenbräu's up to, Devil?" the girl asked, turning her back on Tommy.

"His duty, maybe," the Texian replied.

"Who for?" Di demanded, restraining her impulse to look at the man in question as both her companions were apparently ignoring him.

"There are some who might say the best way to find out is to go over and ask," Ole Devil stated. "Shall I do just that, Tommy?"

"Humble self considers it would be best," the little Oriental agreed.

"Now just you hold hard there for a teensy minute!" Di ordered. "Leave us not forget's how you've sent off half of your boys to help get Grandpappy Ewart and them other wounded fellers' hurts tended to. Top of that, all of Tom Wolf's scouts didn't go with 'em are standing guard too far off to get back 'n' help us very quick."

Having questioned the *mozos*[7] of two Mexican officers who had been taken prisoner during the fighting, Ole Devil had learned that the remaining seven companies of the Arizona Hopi Activos Regiment were camped about two days' ride to the south, awaiting their colonel's return. That had meant they would be unable to put in an appearance for some considerable time.

Faced with the possibility of further trouble and dissension between the two outfits, Ole Devil had seen how the information would allow him to prevent it. Selecting the hotheads from Company C, he had sent them under Lieutenant Mannen Blaze to escort the wounded as far as Washington-on-the-Brazos. A protesting Beauregard Rassendyll had been dispatched with the others, along with four of the Tejas Indians who were serving as scouts for the mule train. This had solved one problem. However, even counting the packers,

7. *Mozo:* a manservant, particularly one employed in a menial capacity.

the force at his command and upon which he could certainly depend was now smaller than the company of dragoons.

"I haven't forgotten," Ole Devil said quietly. "But I was hoping that von Löwenbräu might have."

4

I'M ASSUMING COMMAND, CAPTAIN HARDIN

Major Ludwig von Löwenbräu scanned the faces of the Red River Volunteer Dragoons contingent as he addressed them and sought for signs as to how they were receiving his comments. All in all, their response was about what he had anticipated.

Knowing his subordinates to be typical of the kind of men who had joined Colonel Frank Johnson's enterprise, the Prussian had selected arguments which he believed would appeal to them. Like himself, the majority were hard-bitten opportunists and regarded the proposed invasion as a chance to obtain loot while they were with the Republic of Texas's main body. So he reminded them of the wealthy seaports which were their objectives on their march south along the coast road. The rest of the men were similar in nature and attitude to the participant of the previous day's knife fight, who was still resentful over his treatment at Ole Devil Hardin's hands. Fiercely patriotic in a misguided way, made overconfident by the Texians' earlier victories, they regarded General Samuel Houston's strategic withdrawal as a cowardly and needless flight.

By playing upon the greed of the opportunists and the desire for more positive action on behalf of the patriots, von Löwenbräu hoped that he would sway them to his purpose. However, being a fair judge of human nature, he was aware that there could be one major obstacle to achieving control of the consignment. Having anticipated it, he had also taken steps to circumvent it.

"Talking about Hardin, Major," Sergeant Otis remarked, at the conclusion of his superior's reminder that the dragoons and not the men of the Texas Light Cavalry had been placed in the position of greatest danger during the fighting. "What'll *he* do when you tell him you're fixing to take the rifles?"

"*Do!*" von Löwenbräu repeated, scowling at the interruption and its maker's somewhat mocking demeanor. "What can he do?"

"Could be we'll soon find out," the noncom declared, before the Prussian could repeat an earlier reminder that he not only was the senior officer present but also had the greater number of men to enforce his orders. "He's headed this way right now."

Letting out a short, savage hiss, von Löwenbräu stiffened slightly. For a moment, controlling his anger with an effort, he glared at Otis's surly features. Then he directed a quick glance around at the faces of the other dragoons, confirming something which he had envisaged from the beginning.

Silently promising himself that he would repay the noncom's disrespectful actions later, the Prussian turned almost as smartly as if he were on a parade ground. He gave the ramrod-straight figure who was approaching only a brief look before sweeping the surrounding area with his gaze. From all appearances, Hardin had not attached any special significance to the dragoons assembling. Standing with her back to the Prussian, Di Brindley was talking to the mule packer Hardin had been watching. Although the little "Chinaman" was walking away, it was not in the direction of the cavalrymen who were making preparations to move out. Instead, he appeared to be heading for the fire around which the girl, both officers, and he had slept the previous night.

Returning his attention to the satanic-faced young Texian, von Löwenbräu could find nothing to suggest his motives might have been suspected. Hardin advanced with the somewhat gasconading swagger which characterized his normal movements. He still had the cloak coat hanging from his shoulders. Satisfied with what he saw, the Prussian dipped his right hand into his jacket's pocket, and it emerged holding a large key.

Although noticing von Löwenbräu's action, Ole Devil was more interested in the men behind him. They had gathered in three closely packed ranks. Every one of them held his rifle, but the weapons were in positions neither of threat nor even readiness. Instead, the dragoons lounged in attitudes of those awaiting developments.

"Di says her men will be ready to move out in fifteen minutes, Major," Ole Devil announced as he came to a halt about twenty feet in front of the Prussian.

"That's good!" von Löwenbräu replied, tapping the key against his left palm as if doing so were nothing more than a nervous habit. "I am assuming command, Captain Hardin. You will consider yourself under my orders."

"I see," Ole Devil drawled, his eyes on the Prussian's face. "And what might your orders be?"

"They are those which brought me here," von Löwenbräu answered, searching the other's face in the hope of learning the thoughts behind it. "To take the consignment of arms to where they will be most usefully employed."

"Where would that be?" Ole Devil challenged.

"In the hands of men who are willing and ready to fight against the enemy," the Prussian stated, pitching his voice so it reached the men to his rear as well as the slim young Texian. "Not being carried by an army which is running away and may discard them if pressed too hard."

"I thought that you'd decided to do your duty to Texas and

join General Houston," Ole Devil remarked, showing no emotion at what had obviously been an insult.

"I might have considered it until I saw how you placed my men's life in jeopardy to save casualties among your own," von Löwenbräu replied, once again hoping to prod the Texian into a hostile response. "That is the kind of action which one might expect from an officer who is willing to run instead of stand and fight."

"With respect, Major, I hardly think you're in a position to judge my conduct in action," Ole Devil countered, and his attitude was still one of deadly calm. "Your injury occurred too early in the action for you to have been able to form any opinion of how I comported myself under fire."

"That is neither here nor there!" von Löwenbräu barked, glaring in an attempt to stare the Texian down. "I am taking charge of the consignment!"

There were, as the Prussian appreciated, disadvantages in continuing a discussion on the previous day's attack. He had made the insulting comments with the object of producing a response which would justify the measures he was contemplating. However, the answer he had received could cost him more than he might gain. Despite his reminders of how they had been placed in the forefront of the battle, he knew his men were still impressed by its successful outcome. So he had no wish to let them hear further references about how he had been incapacitated shortly after the commencement of hostilities, while Hardin had taken a prominent part from the beginning to the end.

"On whose authority?" Ole Devil challenged, using tones of icy politeness and meeting the other's eyes without flinching.

"On the authority granted by my commission as a major in the army of the Republic of Texas," von Löwenbräu explained, grateful for the opportunity to establish that he had what could be regarded as a legitimate right to make the demand. "Which makes me your superior in rank. What is more, *Captain* Hardin, as you have seen fit to send off more than half of your company, my men form the bulk of the escort, and that places the responsibility for the consignment's safe delivery on their shoulders." He paused for a few seconds to let the dragoons absorb his words and wished he could look back to find out how they were being received. "You can have a choice, *Captain*. Come with us and play a part in carrying the war to the enemy, or take your men and join General Houston in his flight."

"Leaving the caplocks with you?"

"Of course!"

"You realize that they were purchased by our supporters in the United States to help us establish our right to form an independent republic?"

"I do," von Löwenbräu admitted. "And I'm sure that our supporters will want them put to the purpose for which they were intended, used to fight against the enemy and not given to men who are running away. Colonel Johnson—"

"Is acting contrary to General Houston's orders," Ole Devil interrupted. "If you wish to continue serving him, that is your affair. But I intend to carry out the duty to which I've been assigned and deliver the consignment."

"Do you know the consequences of refusing to obey the orders of a lawfully appointed superior while on active service?" von Löwenbräu demanded, stepping two militarily smart paces nearer to the Texian and keeping all his attention upon him.

"I do," Ole Devil admitted, standing as motionless as if he were made of stone.

"You know that you can be shot, without the need for a court-martial to pronounce sentence, if you refuse to obey?"

"Yes."

"Then, Captain Hardin!" the Prussian barked, standing at a rigid brace so that his right hand—holding the bulky key with its oval grip on his palm and its stem between the first and second fingers—was pointing to the ground. "By the authority granted from my commission as a major of the

Republic of Texas, I *order* you to place yourself and the consignment of arms under my command."

"I refuse," Ole Devil answered, with no greater show of emotion than if he had been involved in a casual and innocuous conversation.

Got you! von Löwenbräu thought exultantly, and without taking his gaze from the Mephistophelian features, he started to raise his right hand.

Considering himself an excellent tactician, the Prussian was delighted at the way he had led his victim into his trap. He had realized from the beginning that talk alone would not gain the dragoons' support. In fact, he had appreciated that he must deal with the other officer before he could hope to achieve his ends. So he had conceived his strategy accordingly. Killing Hardin would present the dragoons with a *fait accompli*. They would be even more willing to back him up against the cavalrymen now he had established, at least to their satisfaction, that he had the authority and legal right to carry out the "execution."

The means by which von Löwenbräu intended to implement his plan had served him most satisfactorily on four previous occasions. Made by a master firearms manufacturer in Germany, the device was a refinement on the key pistols of earlier generations, which had been produced for jailers and others who might require a dual-purpose unsuspected weapon. Designed to operate on the percussion system, it was more compact than its predecessors and was lethal at the distance which separated him from his victim. What was more, as he had not shown it to anybody who was present, he felt sure that he alone appreciated its deadly purpose.

Unfortunately for the Prussian, Ole Devil had come across references to key-pistols in various books about firearms he had read. So he had guessed what the other had in mind when he had seen the device emerging from the pocket. In addition, the trend taken by the conversation had suggested how von Löwenbräu was meaning to kill him. With the safety

of the consignment as an added inducement, he had decided
how he would counter the attempt.

Just as the Prussian had not been required to produce the
disguised weapon during the battle with the Hopis, there had
been no cause for Ole Devil to demonstrate a fighting technique which he had developed. Even before he had come to
Texas, he had considered that the *defensive* qualities of a
pistol were not being fully utilized by the accepted methods
of the day. So, after considerable thought and experimenta-
tion, he had found a means by which such a weapon could be
carried upon the person, then produced and fired with considerable speed.

Realizing that his refusal would present von Löwenbräu
with an excuse to use the key-pistol, Ole Devil did not need
to watch for its being elevated in his direction. Instead, an
instant after he had spoken, he sprang to his left. Simultaneously his right hand turned palm outward and enfolded the
butt of the Manton pistol. Then, employing similar actions to
those which would be used by a later generation of gunfighters when performing a high cavalry-twist draw,[1] he started to
slide the barrel from the retaining loop of his belt.

With the key-pistol rising into alignment, the Prussian became aware that his would-be victim was moving aside. Furious over the discovery that he had been overconfident, he
tried to correct his aim. However, he was unable to halt the
pressure he had begun to exert upon the stud on the back of
the grip which served as a trigger. There was a sharp crack,
and a .41 caliber round lead ball passed through the disguised weapon's short barrel.

In spite of having made the correct deductions, Ole Devil
had almost left his evasion too late. Von Löwenbräu's ball
passed through the material of his cloak coat beneath the

1. A detailed description of the later technique for performing the high
cavalry-twist draw, the major difference being that the hammer was
cocked by the thumb of the hand holding the weapon, is given in *Slip
Gun*.

bent right arm as it was turning the muzzle of the Manton outward. Despite feeling the slight tug, he refused to let himself become flustered by the narrow escape. Already his left hand was crossing to hook over and draw the hammer.

Held at waist level, aimed by instinct and without the need to look along the sights, the pistol bellowed almost as soon as Ole Devil landed from the leap that had saved his life. For all that, guided by the skill acquired through long hours of practice, the heavy bullet flew true. Rising, it entered beneath the Prussian's jaw and retained sufficient power to smash its way out of the top of his skull. He was killed instantly, the key-pistol slipping from his grasp. The men behind him jumped hurriedly out of the way as he crashed backward to the ground.

Startled exclamations burst from the dragoons. Even when they had seen Ole Devil approaching without showing any signs of suspecting the purpose of their gathering, none of them had expected that he would yield to von Löwenbräu's commands. Nor had they anticipated how the Prussian was meaning to terminate the affair. So the sudden eruption of violence caught them unawares.

"All right, Sergeant Otis," Ole Devil said, before any of the startled men could recover their wits, as he allowed the smoking pistol to dangle downward at his side, "the matter's settled, and the consignment is going to General Houston. Have the major buried and be ready to move out as soon as the mules are loaded."

For all the calm and apparently assured manner in which he was speaking, the Texian was studying the dragoons' reactions with well-concealed anxiety. Like von Löwenbräu, he believed that the enlisted men were content to allow their officers to settle the matter of who was in command between themselves and would go along with the winner. If he was wrong, the threat to the consignment was still far from ended, and the danger to his own life was even greater than when he had confronted the Prussian. Not only had he lost the element of surprise, but he was holding an empty pistol, and if his instructions had been carried out by Di and Tommy, his friends were in no position to come to his aid quickly enough to save him.

Listening to the crisply delivered and seemingly confident orders, the dragoons ceased to center their attention on the Texian and his victim. Up to that point, as Ole Devil had hoped, they had been too engrossed in him and the Prussian to watch what the other occupants of the hollow were doing. Although the latter were all looking toward them, none were making any attempt to approach or even draw weapons. In fact, with three exceptions, they began to carry on with their work as if satisfied that the situation was under control.

Even the exceptions were neither displaying concern nor offering to arm themselves. The girl was standing with her hands on her hips but had moved until she was at the center of the packers' activities. Although Tommy had collected his bow in passing and had joined Sergeant Smith at the Texas Light Cavalry's horse lines, there was no arrow nocked to its string. Instead, he and the noncom's attitudes conveyed the impression that they considered the trouble over and that no action on their part would be required.

Bringing back his gaze to Ole Devil, Sergeant Otis sucked in a deep breath. Of all his party, he was the most perturbed by the way the situation had developed. Once again he had been singled out and put into a position of responsibility. He did not like the sensation any more than he had on the previous occasion.

Although Otis felt no personal loyalty toward Colonel Johnson, he could see the advantages of carrying out the orders which had caused von Löwenbräu's death. Not only would taking part in the invasion be less dangerous than joining the main body of the army, but it was certain to be a much more lucrative proposition. Considering the latter point, he knew that promotion would come his way if he delivered the caplocks, and he felt sure the officers would receive the pick of the loot.

With the major dead, Otis knew that the rest of the

dragoons would follow his lead. So, if he was to make a bid for control of the consignment, the numerical odds were still in his favor. In addition, his companions had weapons more readily available than those of the cavalrymen. All he had to do was give the order—

And contend with Captain Hardin's opposition to accepting it.

That, the burly noncom warned himself, was the main snag in attempting to take over von Löwenbräu's assignment. He remembered all too well how the young captain had circumvented other schemes to acquire the caplocks.

Despite Hardin's clearly having suspected treachery, the cavalrymen and the Tejas packers were not making any preparations to defend the consignment. He would not have overlooked such a basic precaution unless he had organized some other means of protecting it.

What if, having mistrusted the Prussian's offer to accompany him, Hardin had only pretended to send half of his men away?

Was the absent party waiting on the rim, ready to take action if the need arose?

Or had Hardin something else in mind?

Watching the sergeant's surly face, which was more expressive than von Löwenbräu's had been, Ole Devil could read his indecision. In spite of it, the Texian's gamble was far from being won. Guessing that the Prussian would have tried to stir up rivalry between the dragoons and his own men, he had told Di and Tommy to prevent the latter from making anything which might be interpreted as a hostile gesture. Concentrating upon Otis, he could not look around and find out if he had kept the conversation with von Löwenbräu going for long enough to let them pass on his instructions. However, if the dragoons' lack of activity was any guide, the girl and the little Oriental had succeeded. That meant his men were not holding weapons, whereas the dragoons had rifles in their hands.

Everything depended upon Otis. If he accepted Ole Devil's orders, his companions would do the same.

A good thirty seconds went by in silence, and although nothing showed on his features, Ole Devil appreciated the problem which was confronting him. The longer the delay, the greater the risk that the sergeant would conclude he had too much in his favor to yield. Yet to try to force the issue before Otis had reached a decision might make him fight out of stubbornness.

"We don't have all day, Sergeant!" Ole Devil stated, knowing that a continued hesitation on his part could be construed as a sign of weakness. "I'd be obliged if you'll put your men to work."

While speaking, the Texian was alert for Otis's first warning flicker of expression. He was ready to drop the empty pistol and draw the bowie knife as swiftly as possible but hoped the need to do so would not arise. If it did, the affair was likely—in fact, would almost certainly—erupt into a clash between the two factions.

There was an interruption before Otis could make his choice.

"Riders coming down, Cap'n Hardin!" Sergeant Smith called.

With a sensation of relief, Otis watched the coldly satanic features—which had been holding his eyes like iron filings drawn to a magnet—turn away. Looking in the direction indicated by Smith, he let out a startled exclamation. The three men who were approaching along the path from the rim were acquaintances and showed signs of having pushed their horses very hard. One of them was his predecessor as sergeant, who had been driven away by Ole Devil during von Löwenbräu's first abortive attempt to take possession of the consignment. It was unlikely that he would have dared return unless confident that it was safe for him to do so.

"What do you make of them, Sergeant Otis?" Ole Devil inquired, having matched the other's identification and analysis.

"They belong to our outfit—sir," the noncom answered, continuing to study the trio as they came closer and drawing a conclusion from their attitudes which suggested he might be advised to use the honorific.

"Hey, fellers!" yelled the former sergeant, before any more could be said. "The Mexican Army's jumped Colonel Johnson down at San Patricio. They've wiped him 'n' all his men out."

5
HELL, WE CAN DO WITHOUT YOU

"It's this way, Cap'n," Sergeant Otis said hesitantly, throwing a glance over his shoulder as if to ensure that the rest of the Red River Volunteer Dragoons contingent was still standing behind him. "Most of these fellers've got homes down San Patricio way, and they're worried about their families."

"That's to be expected," Ole Devil Hardin replied in a noncommittal tone.

Knowing the request he was going to make, and having learned the nature of the man to whom it would be addressed, the burly noncom sought for some indication of how his words were being received. He met with little success. Standing ramrod straight, legs apart and hands behind his back, the young officer revealed nothing of his thoughts.

For all his impassive exterior, Ole Devil had a very good idea of what was coming. Over the past few minutes, despite having been occupied in another matter, he had noticed certain things which had helped him to draw his conclusions.

Although the news which was received too late to save Major Ludwig von Löwenbräu from death had removed the most immediate threat to Ole Devil's mission, he would have preferred it to have been delivered in a more discreet fashion. Not unexpectedly, learning of their companions' misfortunes had had a disturbing and demoralizing effect upon the dragoons, and he had appreciated that far from removing the problems with which he was faced, the tiding had added to them.

Passing on the information to Diamond Hitch Brindley, Tommy Okasi, and Sergeant Smith, Ole Devil had sent them to continue with the preparations for moving out. Then he had given his attention to the newcomers. The presence of a second Mexican column north of the Rio Grande, particularly as it was coming from an unanticipated quarter, could pose a very serious threat to Major General Samuel Houston's policy of withdrawal. So Ole Devil wanted to have a better understanding of the situation before he took any action.

Unfortunately, in spite of having subjected the two dragoons to a lengthy questioning, Ole Devil had not improved his knowledge of what had happened at San Patricio to any great extent. It had soon become apparent that the pair had thought only of saving their own skins. Neither had been able to say which, or even how many, Mexican regiments had been employed to defeat Colonel Frank Johnson's command. Even the number of attackers they had claimed to be involved had struck him as being wildly exaggerated. What was more, unless he was mistaken, their arrival at Santa Cristóbal Bay had come about more through a chance meeting with Otis's predecessor than from a desire to do their duty by delivering a warning. About the only positive information they could give was that to the best of their knowledge, they had not been pursued in their flight.

Throughout the interrogation Ole Devil had been aware that the other dragoons were not making ready to leave. Instead, they had gathered around Otis and his predecessor, talking volubly and quietly with many glances at him. Nor had he been surprised when, having dismissed the survivors, the noncom had approached him, displaying a somewhat apprehensive demeanor.

"Then you'll likely see's how we don't feel it'd be right for us to go heading off away from 'em when they're going to be in danger," Otis went on, wishing that the other's cold black eyes would look away from him. "It's— Well— We— They're—"

"Get to the point, Sergeant," Ole Devil requested, giving no indication that he knew what it would be. "There's still plenty to be done before we can pull out."

"Th—that's what I want to talk to you about, sir," Otis replied, shuffling his feet and dropping his gaze to the ground. "Us fellers— Well, we're all of a mind to go back and take care of our families. All of us feel tolerable strong about it—sir. So, happen it's all right with you?"

"Very well, Sergeant," Ole Devil drawled when the noncom's words trailed to a halt. Apparently paying no attention to the group of dragoons who hovered with sullenly menacing attitudes in the background, he continued, "You can go!"

"It's not that we wan—" Otis began, before an understanding of how his request had been treated sank in. "Huh?"

"I said that you can go back, instead of coming with us," Ole Devil explained. "There's only one thing I'd like you to do for me. Wait until after we've gone, bury Major von Löwenbräu, and make sure that we haven't left anything down here that would tell the Mexicans what we've been doing."

"Sure thing, Cap'n!" Otis replied, so relieved at having received permission to leave the escort duty that he gave the agreement without hesitation. A quicker thinker might have wondered why the request had been made. The boxes in which the caplocks were delivered had been burned, and the Mexicans already knew they had arrived. "We'll tend to everything here for you. I'm right sorry to be leaving you shorthanded this ways, but—"

"Don't let *that* bother you, Sergeant," Ole Devil interrupted. "I told Mr. Blaze to come back as soon as they'd seen the wounded safely across the San Bernard River. They'll be meeting us before we've gone much more than a mile."

"I'm right pleased to hear it, Cap'n," Otis declared, having suspected that such an arrangement had been made and believing the second party of the Texas Light Cavalry was even closer so as to help deal with any treachery his late superior had been contemplating. "Looks like you won't have any trouble getting them caplocks to General Houston even with us gone."

"*You* can count on it that we won't, Sergeant," Ole Devil stated, with an air of grimly determined finality. "And I hope that you all find your families safe when you reach San Patricio."

With that, the young officer strode past the dragoons. For all the notice he took of them, they might not have existed. Showing relief, mingled with puzzlement, Otis swung around and watched him go.

"What'd he say?" demanded the former sergeant as his replacement walked up.

"We can go," Otis replied.

"I told you he wouldn't dare try to stop us," scoffed the former noncom.

"I wouldn't want to count on it," Otis warned. "He wants us to stay on, bury von Löwenbräu, and clean up after the mule train's pulled out, and I said we would."

"Why should we?" protested one of the dragoons.

"Because that's what *he* wants, and I don't figure to rile him by saying no," Otis answered, scowling at his companions. "Like I warned you, the rest of his company's close enough by to take cards real fast should they be needed. So we're staying down here until after they've gone well out of sight and won't find out which way we're really heading."

"Aw, hell!" objected Wilkie, fingering the hilt of his knife sulkily. "This don't set right with me. We ain't doing nothing to pay them greasers back for what happened to the rest of our boys."

"It might not set right to some, but it makes right good sense to me," growled the taller of the survivors. "I know what happened down to San Patricio. Them guys who wiped out our fellers'll be headed up here foot, hoss 'n' artillery. 'Twixt them and Santa Anna, we don't stand a snowball in hell's chance. The only way out's to head for the good ole U.S. of A. afore we gets caught in the middle."

"Thing being," put in another of the original dragoons company, "I'm like you 'n' most of the others, Wilkie, got folks up along the Red. So I aims to see 'em safe instead of trying to get evens for somebody's already dead, 'specially when there ain't enough of us to do nothing should we try."

"All right then," Otis put in, after a rumble of agreement had died down. "We're headed north. Only, seeing's how we've got Hardin fooled, let's keep him that way by doing what he's asked. Hell, we can rest up until noon at least and still be on our way afore there's any chance of the Texians catching up with us."

Sharing the noncom's opinion of how dangerous the Mephistophelian-faced young officer could be when roused or crossed, the rest of the dragoons were willing to accept his suggestions. They all felt that their flight would be much easier to accomplish now they had tricked Ole Devil Hardin over their true purpose for leaving the mule train.

If the dragoons had overheard the conversation which took place between the Texian when he had joined Di Brindley and Tommy Okasi, they would have discovered that they had been far from successful in their deception.

Crossing to where Di was talking to Tommy, Ole Devil noticed with satisfaction that the various preparations for departure were progressing. His men and the mule packers had been interested in the newcomers, but Sergeant Smith and Joe Galton had not let them be diverted from their respective tasks.

For her part, the girl had watched the interview between

Ole Devil and Otis. She also noticed that although it had ended, the latter and his men were still standing in a group. However, her main attention was upon the young Texian. During the time they had been together and shared a number of dangers, she had learned a lot about him. Sufficient for her to wonder why he was allowing the dragoons to behave in such a manner instead of insisting that they got on with their work.

"Likely it's none of my never-mind," Di remarked as Ole Devil joined her, "but happen those butt-trailing yahoos don't right soon start to saddling up, they'll not be ready to move out with us."

"It doesn't matter if they aren't," the Texian answered, with no more emotion than he had shown while talking to Otis. "We're leaving them here."

"Huh!" the girl snorted, and the glance she directed at the dragoons showed anything but faith in their abilities. "I can't say's it makes me feel a whole heap safer knowing it's them's'll be 'tween us and any Mexicans's're coming."

"I wouldn't let *that* worry you," Ole Devil replied. "They won't be. Sergeant Otis told me that they're all so worried about the folks they've left behind that they're heading down to San Patricio to effect a rescue. So I wished them the best of luck with it and said they could go."

"You *believed* them?" Di yelped.

"If you must know," Ole Devil said calmly, "I didn't."

"Then why in hell—" the girl spluttered.

"Because, with the mood they're in, they'd desert en masse if I'd said they couldn't go," Ole Devil explained, seeming to grow calmer as Di's indignation increased. "And I've neither the time nor the inclination to stop them, even if it could be done. The frame of mind they're in, we couldn't count on them to stand by us if the Mexicans catch up with the train."

"You could be right at that," the girl conceded, considering the alarm being shown by the Dragoons. Then she glared at Tommy, who was clearly about to speak, warning, "And I don't want any of them son-of-a-bitching wise old whatever-they-are sayings that you've just made up from *you*."

"Humble self was only going to point out how when danger threatens, it is wiser to depend upon a few warriors who are steadfast than to have many who will run at the sight of the enemy," the little Oriental commented, exuding patience and forebearance. "Fear is like a contagious sickness. It goes from one who has it to those who have not and infects them."

"Them's a right fancy heap of words to say nothing." The girl sniffed with well-simulated disdain, although she had understood and agreed with all Tommy had said. However, having no intention of admitting that she did, she returned her attention to the third member of their group. "Just how bad are things down to San Patricio?"

"I wish I knew for sure," Ole Devil answered, and something in his voice confirmed Di's suspicions that he regarded the news as exceedingly grave. "According to the two men who came here, all of Johnson's command have gone under except for themselves."

"That being the case, we'd best send off word to General Sam," the girl suggested, despite feeling certain the point had already occurred to her companion. "If all of 'em have been made wolf bait, neither him nor Fannin's boys over to Goliad'll have heard what's happened."

"Sending a message based on the little I've learned could do more harm than good," Ole Devil said quietly, but still giving Di an inkling of the problem with which he was faced. "I might be doing those two an injustice, but I think they ran away from San Patricio before the fighting was over. Things might not be as bad as they've made out."

"You mean that Johnson's bunch could've fought off the Mexicans after they'd run away?" Di asked.

"It's a possibility," Ole Devil replied. "And even if they were beaten, those two might not be the only survivors. In which case, somebody could already have taken the news to Goliad."

"Somebody *might* have," Di admitted, instinctively appreciating the misgivings which were plaguing the Texian. "Only, from what I've seen of Johnson's bunch so far, I'd sooner bet's anybody who got clear'd be running north as fast as they could rather than was headed to where the Mexicans'd be likely to go next."

"That's the problem," Ole Devil conceded. "But if I send word based on just what those two told me, there'll be some in the garrison at Goliad and with the general who won't wait to learn how serious the situation might be."

"There's some's won't, happen the way those Red River yahoos've let it spook 'em is anything to go on," the girl admitted, favoring the dragoons with a disgusted look. "And once a few start pulling out, more'll follow. Couldn't you send word to General Sam and make sure that nobody but him gets it?"

"I could try, but doing it wouldn't be advisable," Ole Devil answered. "The effect would be a whole lot worse if it slipped out. That's why I'm going to tell my men all I know before we set off."

Such was the faith that Di had developed where Ole Devil was concerned, it had never occurred to her to wonder how the members of the Texas Light Cavalry who were present might be affected by the news from Goliad and the dragoons' behavior. On the other hand, she could imagine how the tidings would be received by Houston's retreating army and the garrison under Colonel James W. Fannin's indecisive command at Goliad. Morale was already low, and finding themselves threatened with encirclement by the Mexicans might prove the breaking point.

Swinging her gaze in the cavalrymen's direction, the girl saw that they were talking among themselves and pointing at the dragoons. However, for all their interest, they had not allowed it to impede them in the work of saddling the horses ready to move out with the mule train. Nor were any of them offering to go over and satisfy their curiosity by questioning members of the other outfit.

"I'd say's how you don't need to worry about them," Di stated. "And to a half-smart lil country girl like me, seems like the easiest way to find out what's happened at San Patricio'd be send somebody to take a look."

"Some such idea had crossed my mind," Ole Devil admitted.

"Only you're not sure who to send," the girl went on.

"I'm not."

"Sergeant Smith's a pretty smart *hombre*."

"He's also married with a young family, and there's no safe way of gathering the kind of information that's needed."

"On top of which, you figure that *you're* the one who's best suited to get it," Di went on, once again making a shrewd guess at the Texian's thoughts. "And much as I hate to have to say it, you're right. Only you've got these caplocks on your hands."

"I have."

"And even if somebody from Johnson's crowd's was took prisoner and, trying to save his skin, hasn't told about 'em, them Hopis will have?"

"It's possible."

"Well, knowing's the Hopis're already after 'em, they'll not be likely to send anybody else, will they?" Di went on, before Ole Devil could finish his comment.

"Probably not," the Texian answered. "Except that they mightn't know the Hopis are after us."

"Why wouldn't they know?" Di challenged.

"According to the *mozos*, the Hopis came from the west," Ole Devil explained. "Nothing they said suggested they knew there were any other Mexican troops nearer than Santa Anna's army. If so, they don't belong to the column which took San Patricio."

"Then them fellers's whupped Johnson's bunch could figure they're the only Mexicans hereabouts," Di remarked. "And they're likely to send somebody to take the caplocks from us."

"It's more than likely," Ole Devil declared. "They're a tempting prize."

"And if they send," the girl continued, more in a statement than a question, "they'll use enough men to make sure of taking 'em and getting 'em back."

"It's not likely they'll send less than half a regiment of cavalry," Ole Devil admitted.

"Well, then," Di said, with the air of having reached a decisive point, "I don't see's how we're all that much worse off. With that many, same's with the Hopis, we've a good head start and we'll be heading away from them near on's fast as they can move."

"That's true," Ole Devil concurred.

"Then it'll be three days, at the very least, afore they could catch up with us," the girl declared. "And by then we'll be close enough to Thompson's Ferry to count on getting enough help to stand 'em off. So, way I see it, there's nothing to stop you 'n' Tommy heading down toward San Patricio and finding out for yourselves what's happening. Hell, we don't need you pair along to hold our hands, and you won't rest easy until you know."

"I wish it was that easy, Di," Ole Devil said. "But there are more than just the Mexicans and the Hopis for us to consider."

"You mean *that* bunch?" Di snorted, indicating the dragoons with a contempt-filled jerk of a thumb. "Huh! You've got the Injun sign on them—"

"Only I won't be along to make sure it stays on," Ole Devil countered. "And they still have us outnumbered."

"Why not just tell 'em straight that we'll start shooting without waiting to find who all's coming happen anybody comes once we're on our way?" the girl asked.

"If I did, they'd know I didn't believe they meant to go south," Ole Devil replied. "And one lesson I learned real early was never to give a horse, dog, or man cause to think I was scared of him. Which is how they'd regard it, and that could give them bad ideas. No, Di. It's not them I'm worrying over. They'll be too busy running for safety to trouble us. But there're the folks at San Felipe. If they learn how small an escort is left—"

Although the replacement for the dead bell mare had been obtained in the small seaport of San Felipe, Di knew why Ole Devil had misgivings. The population was notorious as unscrupulous cutthroats, some of whom would be only too willing to snap up such valuable loot as the consignment.

"You know something, Devil," the girl said quietly, with a mischievous grin. "After the news they're going to get, I don't reckon's they'll cause us any fuss."

"Which news?"

"Well, now," Di answered, contriving to give off an aura of innocence, "I've just got me a feeling that they're going to get told the same's we've heard about what happened at San Patricio— Except that they'll hear's how the Mexicans's whupped Johnson're already headed north along the coast trail. And once they've been told that, I'm game to bet that the only thing's'll get them away from the boats there'd be to put all they own in a wagon and head for the U.S. line like the devil after a yearling."

"Would it be too much to ask who is going to do this 'telling'?" Ole Devil inquired, hearing Tommy giving a delighted chuckle.

"Tom Wolf," Di answered, naming the chief of her Tejas employees. "And everybody *know*s Injuns don't *never* tell lies. Which it's sure lucky ole Tom's been 'round us white folks long enough to've learned how."

"Around *you* white folks," Ole Devil corrected. "I don't want to be blamed for corrupting him."

Despite the light way in which he had just spoken, the Texian was all too aware that he was in a very difficult position. He was torn between two conflicting duties: the one to which he had been assigned by his commanding general and that of an officer in a light cavalry regiment, a major task of which was the gathering of military information. The situation at San Patricio called for investigation by somebody who was capable of assessing its full potential, and without being immodest, he knew that he was the man best suited to carry out the task. However, the safe delivery of the caplocks and ammunition could make the difference between victory and defeat when Houston made his stand. As in the previous case, he knew that he was the man best suited to ensure the consignment reached its destination.

So Ole Devil had to decide what to do.

And the decision must be correct!

Either way the future of the Republic of Texas might depend upon it!

6
IT DON'T PAY TO LAG
BEHIND

"We're all ready to go, happen you are, Devil," Diamond Hitch Brindley announced, riding up as the young Texian was walking away from the Red River Volunteer Dragoons after having taken part in an impromptu funeral service for Major Ludwig von Löwenbräu.

"So are we, Di," Ole Devil Hardin replied, neither his tone nor expression supplying any hint to how he was feeling with regard to the line of action to which he had committed himself. Raising his voice, he called, "Mount the company, Sergeant Smith."

"Yo!" the noncom answered, and gave the requisite order.

Darting a glance filled with disgust at the men who were gathered around the grave, Di needed all her self-control to hold back the comments she felt bubbling inside her. None of the men met her scornful gaze, and remembering Ole Devil's desire to avoid letting them know that their true purpose was suspected, she turned her horse away without addressing them.

"All right, Joe!" the girl yelled, keeping pace with the satanic-featured Texian and waving a hand to the *cargador*.

"I've got the soldier boys woke up. Now you can start *our* knob-heads moving."

Turning her gaze to the ramrod-straight figure striding alongside her, Di found he was watching what was going on around him. Although she noticed that his attention was directed toward the activities of her men rather than his own, she felt no resentment. She knew why he was taking such interest.

Fortunately for Ole Devil, in the course of his far from uneventful young life he had cultivated a fatalistic outlook. When faced with problems, even the most demanding upon which important issues might depend, he had learned to give them careful consideration before taking action. However, once having reached a decision and taken whatever precautions he believed would contribute to success—making the fullest use of such resources as he had available—he was aware of the danger of indulging in self-doubt. And he did his best to avoid fretting over the consequences if it was proved that his judgment had been at fault. He had always been helped in this by being blessed with an inquiring mind, which would never cease trying to add to its fund of knowledge, and he could generally find something of interest to help divert his attention from whatever cares might be assailing him.

So, having planned how to cope with his current difficulties, the young Texian was finding that traveling with the Brindleys' mule train was proving to be something of a blessing. While fully cognizant of how vitally important it was for him to ensure that the consignment did not fall into the wrong hands, at the same time the means by which it was being transported served to prevent him from being plagued by concern over the various perturbing aspects arising from the decision he had taken. He believed that he was acting in the most suitable manner, but he also realized that he was relying upon insufficient and possibly inaccurate information.

Like every officer carrying out an independent assignment

in the days before the invention of rapid means of communication—such as, for example, the radio—Ole Devil appreciated that he was out of touch with the current situation elsewhere.[1] So he was compelled to rely upon his own initiative and summations based upon the last-known state of affairs.

When Ole Devil had set off with orders to collect and deliver the consignment, the main body of the Republic of Texas's army had been about to fall back to the town of Gonzales on the Guadalupe River. However, as Presidente Antonio López de Santa Anna had already crossed the Rio Grande, a detachment of 182 volunteers under the joint command of Colonels William Barrett Travis, James Bowie, and David ("Davy") Crockett had insisted upon staying in the Alamo Mission at San Antonio de Béxar. It was their intention to try to delay *el presidente* for long enough to allow Major General Samuel Houston to consolidate the rest of the Texians' forces. They were to be reinforced by some of the 400 well-armed and -equipped men, under the command of Colonel James Walker Fannin, occupying Fort Defiance at Goliad.

Although that was practically the sum of Ole Devil's knowledge, he was working on the assumption that no news from the main body was good news. He felt sure that if some major catastrophe had befallen them, General Houston would have found a way of notifying him so that he could dispose of the consignment and prevent embarrassment to their supporters in the United States. For all that, the information which had arrived from San Patricio was adding a

1. A classic example of the effect of slow communications occurred during the final stages of the American Civil War. The last engagement, ironically won by a unit of the Confederate States army under the command of Colonel John Salmon "Rip" Ford, took place at Palmitto Hill, about fifteen miles east of Brownsville, Cameron County, Texas, on May 13, 1865, more than a month *after* the surrender of General Robert E. Lee at the Appomattox Courthouse in Virginia—on April 9—should have brought an end to military hostilities.

new dimension to his problems, and he had taken it into account when selecting his future movements.

While approving of Di's suggestion for reducing the possibility of trouble from the less scrupulous citizens of San Felipe, Ole Devil had also been aware that in all probability any attempt they might be contemplating would already have been set into motion. In addition, after having been deprived of the chance of loot from other sources, the surviving members of Colonel Frank Johnson's ill-fated command might try to compensate themselves by gaining possession of at least some of the valuable caplock rifles and ammunition.

Without being egotistical, the Texian had appreciated that he had established a very healthy respect for himself among the members of both factions. His presence with the mule train was likely to serve as a strong deterrent to any plans they might be considering. In the event of an attack by either group, his planning ability and guidance would do much to offset whatever disparity in numbers there was between his party and the attackers.

Taking everything into account, Ole Devil was inclined to regard the enemy as being the least pressing factor as far as the protection of the consignment was concerned. Di had made a sound point when stating that the mules could, even if unable to outrun any pursuers, at least make the chase such a lengthy affair that there would be a good chance of their reaching an area in which reinforcements could be obtained before they were overtaken.

Against that, the Texian was faced with the problem of finding out exactly what had happened at San Patricio and learning everything possible about the strength and intentions of the second column. On thinking about it, he concluded that there might not be any extreme urgency for an investigation. From what he had seen of Mexicans, and Di—whose knowledge of them was even more extensive—had agreed, he doubted whether the victors could resist celebrating their success over Johnson's command. In that case, they were unlikely to take any further military action until the

festivities were at an end. Even then their soundest tactics—
and probably their orders—would be to move westward and,
having dealt with the garrison at Fort Defiance, try to trap
the main body of Houston's army between themselves and
Santa Anna's force.

In that case, unless the second column sent a detachment
north in the hope of snapping up such a tempting prize, they
did not pose too great a threat to the consignment. Nor,
even if there were no other survivors from the fighting at San
Patricio, were they likely to catch the garrison at Fort Defiance unawares. Fannin might not be an efficient and ener-
getic commanding officer, but his instinct for self-preserva-
tion was such that he would have patrols operating in his
immediate vicinity. Even if he did not, he had officers serving with him—such as Captain James Butler Bonham[2]—who
would ensure that such a basic military precaution was carried out.

Despite his conclusion, Ole Devil had known he would
have no peace of mind until he had personally reviewed the
situation. So he had reached what he regarded as a satisfactory compromise to deal with his dilemma. He would accompany the mule train as far as the San Bernard River, beyond
which he had felt sure there would be no danger from either
the dragoons or the citizens of San Felipe. Then, provided
nothing else had come up, he and Tommy Okasi would return and carry out a reconnaissance in the direction of San
Patricio.

Once Ole Devil had made up his mind, he informed his
companions of his decision. Then, while the packers were
completing the preparations for departure, he told his men
about the news from San Patricio and that the dragoons

2. After failing to persuade Colonel Fannin to reinforce the Alamo Mission and, having penetrated the surrounding Mexican lines, after delivering a warning that no help would be forthcoming, Captain James Butler
Bonham (1807–1836) elected to remain and perished with the other defenders on March 6.

would no longer be accompanying them. As he had anticipated, the men of the Texas Light Cavalry were not dis-
tressed to learn of Johnson's downfall. Nor were they perturbed to discover that the size of the escort would be
drastically reduced. Their view was that the dragoons would
be no great loss. Although none of them had mentioned it,
he could tell that they were sharing his own suspicions over
the reason Sergeant Otis had given for leaving.

Having had a grave dug, Otis had requested that Ole Devil
perform the burial service over the dead Prussian. Wanting
to convince the dragoons that he had no doubts about them,
the young officer agreed. With that task completed and having nothing further demanding his immediate attention, he
was looking forward with eager anticipation to the commencement of the journey. Not only did he want to have the
consignment on the move, but he wished to learn more
about the way in which the mule train was handled.

In the past when Ole Devil had had occasion to make use
of pack animals, they had always been horses. Mostly he had
employed them singly, and he had never had more than half
a dozen to contend with.

When conditions called for a number of horses to be used,
they could be led individually or, provided they were trained
for the work and traversing a good trail which had few ob-
structions such as fallen trees or deep streams, fastened one
behind the other. The latter arrangement was carried out by
either securing the lead rope to the "back buck" of the packsaddle of the horse in front or by "tailing" them in line.
Whichever method was selected, each led animal had to be
far enough behind the horse it was following so that it could
not be kicked, but sufficiently close to prevent it from stepping over a dangling lead rope and becoming entangled. This
limited the number of animals that could be coupled up to
form a string, and it was inadvisable to secure more than
four together.

Where possible, tailing was the more satisfactory method.
This was carried out by half hitching a metal ring to the

preceding horse's tail. The next in line's lead rope was attached to it by a short length of quarter-inch cord or by a double thickness of hay bale twine, either of which would break easily in an emergency. On the other hand, wherein lay tailing's main advantage, if something happened to startle a horse that was being led by the back buck, its struggles might snatch off its predecessor's saddle or even bring them both down.

Effective as leading by the back buck or tailing method might be when dealing with no more than a handful of horses, Ole Devil realized that neither method was feasible when traveling with the large number of animals required to transport the consignment. However, as Di had explained, over the centuries packers had learned to take advantage of a peculiar trait in the nature of the creatures which they had found most suitable for their purposes.

Despite being hybrids—produced by crossing a male donkey with a female horse[3]—which meant that they were rarely able to procreate and never produced fertile offspring on the rare occasions when they succeeded, mules tended to find the company of a mare irresistible. Packers had discovered that recalcitrant though they might be in some circumstances, they would follow a female horse all day without the need to be led or tailed. Furthermore, when a bell was carried by the mare, its sound apparently produced a soothing effect upon them. In fact, under its comforting influence, they were content to remain close to her through the hours of darkness while on a journey without requiring to be hobbled or secured in any other fashion.

On receiving Di's order, Joe Galton set about utilizing the mules' obsession with the opposite sex. Starting his mount

3. The result of a cross between a horse stallion and a female donkey is called a hinny. Always smaller than a mule, the hinny bears an even closer resemblance to its dam. Inheriting the donkey's obstinate disposition to an even greater degree, which combines with its smaller size to make it a less useful beast of burden, the hinny has never been bred to the same extent as have mules.

moving, a gentle tug on the hackamore's lead rope caused the horse that was fastened to his saddle horn to accompany him as he rode toward the slope.

The replacement, which had been obtained by Di, Ole Devil, and Tommy—at some considerable risk to themselves[4]—was a much finer-looking animal than the Brindleys's original bell mare. However, appearances and physical conformation were not of great importance in the performance of her duties. Her predecessor had been a most unprepossessing creature, unsuitable for either comfortable riding or even the lightest draft work, but this had never detracted from her worth as an essential part of the mule train. When on the move, her only burden had been the hackamore by which she was led and the bell that was suspended from the leather collar around her neck. Fortunately the new animal was of a placid disposition and did not raise any objection to having the clonking of the bell's clapper so close to her. In fact, she had already settled down to her duties in a satisfactory manner.

Hearing the mare's bell and having learned by long experience what to expect when the heavy loads had been placed in position, the majority of the mules began walking after the departing mare. One of the exceptions, a mean-looking, washy brown animal bearing the number 28 on its *corona*, continued to stand as if engrossed in deepest meditation not far from where Ole Devil was passing. Wanting to find out what would happen, he came to a halt and watched. It was one of Prays Loudly, Sometimes' string, and the packer had clearly anticipated something of the sort would take place. Setting his riding mule into motion, he guided it behind the stationary beast. Swinging the doubled-over length of rope he was now carrying, he delivered a couple of hearty whacks to 28's rump and accompanied them with a couple of loudly spoken Anglo-Saxon "cusswords." Giving a snort and shake of its head, but showing neither alarm nor resentment over

4. The events referred to are related in *Ole Devil and the Caplocks*.

such treatment, the mule started to amble after its companions.

Looking around, Ole Devil found that some of the other
packers were engaged in encouraging such of their charges
as were displaying a similar tardiness over joining the march.
Not all of the laggards needed blows to stimulate a willingness to cooperate. A few responded to verbal abuse, either
in Tejas or with English vilifications picked up by the user
without his having troubled to learn more of the language.
The means of physical inducement varied from those who
shared Prays Loudly, Sometimes' faith in a length of rope to
those who favored a bare-handed slap or a kick. However,
the Texian noticed that the target was invariably either the
rump or the ribs. Nor, he also observed, was any punishment
given unless it was warranted, and in every case four blows at
the most, backed where necessary by a volley of obscene
threats, were required to produce the desired result.

"It looks like most of them are as eager as I am to be
getting under way," Ole Devil remarked, glancing up at Di
as she lounged on the saddle of her big bay gelding by his
side.

"Shucks," the girl replied, without interrupting her examination of the way things were progressing. "They all know it
don't pay to lag behind so's they'd have to run afore they
catch up. Only, way some mules act, you've got to sort of jog
their memories afore they remember it. Grandpappy Ewart
allus allows it's them long ears's makes 'em go a touch ab-
sentminded now and then."

For all the Texian's lack of practical experience at packing,
by studying the departing animals, he could guess why it was
essential to prevent any of them from being left too far behind at the start of the march. Once they had commenced
moving, the mules adopted an ambling fox-trot gait which
allowed them to travel without unduly rocking their loads.
Any other pace, whether a fast walk, a jogging trot, or running, would transmit a troublesome motion to the packs.

"I'll say one thing, they weren't any trouble to get moving," Ole Devil commented, recollecting all the stories he had heard about the awkward, stubborn, and uncooperative natures of the species *mulus*. "I've always been told that the only treatment a mule understood was with a firm hand and that the hand should be used to take a grip on a good stout club."

"Not all of 'em," Di contradicted, looking at the Texian. "Mules're like people. Some you can ask polite and they'll do it; others you need to whomp a mite afore they'll oblige. Only, happen you have to work with a club, wham his butt end and not over his head. Mules ain't like you menfolks; you can hurt 'em bad and do damage by whomping 'em between the ears."

"My grandfather Baines always told me that the only time a gentleman should strike a woman is when she's not wearing corsets," Ole Devil stated, as if imparting very important information, meeting the girl's challenging gaze without flinching.

"Why?" Di asked, before she could stop herself.

"It's dangerous to kick her in the stomach when she is," the Texian replied, his demeanor implying that the girl should remember the advice. "He claimed that the one time he forgot and did it, he broke his big toe."

"It's a son-of-a-bitching pity he didn't break his fool neck *afore* he met your grandmammy Baines!" Di snorted. Then, noticing Tommy approaching with Ole Devil's linebacked dun gelding, she pulled a wry face and went on. "I'm going afore *he* gets to spouting some more of them son-of-a-bitching wise old what-in-hell-he-calls-'em sayings. *Some* folks around here've got better things to do than just standing jawing about nothing 'n' looking pretty."

"Well," Ole Devil drawled as the girl started to rein her mount around, "that's one thing nobody could accuse *you* of doing."

"That's for su—" Di commenced, but a sudden realization of how the comment had been worded caused her to bring the bay to a halt and glare at the speaker. "Just which son of a bitch of 'em did you mean?"

"I'll leave *that* for *you* to decide," Ole Devil replied, his attitude conveying a belief that the matter was beneath his attention. He strolled over to meet the little Oriental.

A smile came to the Texian's lips as he listened to the profane prediction which followed him about his most likely future. The lighthearted exchange of banter had helped divert both Di's and his thoughts from their problems. That was useful. In spite of believing that he was carrying out his duties in the best possible manner, he could not help feeling disturbed by the way he would be doing it.

Knowing how anxious the girl was over her grandfather's well-being, Ole Devil had the greatest admiration for her courage and the manner in which she was conducting their family's affairs. She was different from any other member of her sex with whom he was acquainted. However, while anything but a misogynist, he harbored no romantic notions where she was concerned. He belonged to an age and generation which had sound moral standards and a sense of purpose, so did not need to use sexual prowess—which, after all, was within the reach of even the most primitive form of mammal—in an attempt to excuse or replace a lack of more desirable qualities. So, although conscious of her physical attractions, he was equally aware that Ewart Brindley had entrusted her into his care. As far as a man of his upbringing was concerned, that trust was inviolate.

For her part, Di had a greater appreciation of the young Texian's feelings than he suspected. She knew the heavy burden of responsibility he was bearing and realized that she had helped him to forget it, even if only for a few seconds.

Watching Ole Devil striding away, the girl found herself considering how her feelings toward him had changed. Although she had had misgivings about him on their first meeting, they no longer troubled her. At that time she had wondered if he might be nothing more than an arrogant and spoiled young man who held his rank by virtue of a wealthy family's influence. Now she knew better. What was more, she had discerned the humanity beneath his grim and apparently ruthless exterior.

Being a realist, despite Tommy's having told her why Ole Devil had left Louisiana and could not return, Di had no visions of their falling in love and spending the rest of their lives in a state of marital bliss. She did not doubt that they would go their separate ways once the consignment was delivered and suspected that, no matter which way the struggle for independence ended, he would be unlikely to settle down in matrimony for several years.

Giving a sigh, the girl nudged the horse with her heels. The time for levity and daydreaming was over. There was work demanding her attention. Maybe there was no immediate threat to the consignment, but she knew that transporting it was the task for which she was responsible. Leaving Ole Devil to his affairs, she rode after the mule train.

7
THEY'RE SMARTER THAN
I REALIZED

"Sergeant Smith said that I should tell you the company is ready for your inspection, Devil-san," Tommy Okasi reported as his employer strolled up to him.

Looking around the hollow, Ole Devil Hardin was once more filled with gratitude for being blessed with intelligent and capable subordinates who could draw conclusions on what was required and act upon them. Showing the kind of initiative which had earned him very rapid and well-deserved promotion (he had in fact been a private on his arrival at Santa Cristóbal Bay), the noncom had not moved out after the departing mule train. Instead, he had formed up the twenty enlisted men of the Texas Light Cavalry's Company C in a single file. Each of them was standing holding his horse with the right hand and his rifle across the crook of his left arm. They were ideally positioned to counter treachery if the remnants of the Red River Volunteer Dragoons should be contemplating it. Furthermore, the reason which had been given for their action would provide an excuse for them to stay behind until the consignment had passed over the rim.

"*¡Bueno!*" the Texian exclaimed, taking the reins of his

linebacked dun gelding from the little Oriental. Conscious that he was being watched by the dragoons, he went on louder than was necessary. "You can get going while I inspect the men, Tommy."

Leading his horse, while the little Oriental rode away, Ole Devil joined his men. He allowed his reins to fall from his grasp, ground hitching the animal, then walked along the file. By pausing before each man and subjecting him to a careful scrutiny, he contrived to stretch out the period of the subterfuge.

"Look at the son of a bitch playing soldiers," sniffed one of the survivors from San Patricio, watching the "inspection" without any inclination of its true purpose.

"Mister," Sergeant Otis growled, speaking no louder but with savage emphasis, "he's not playing. There's the best goddamned soldier you'll ever see."

"Happen you're so all-fired fond of him," the survivor spit out, "maybe you should be going with him 'stead of us."

"You could be right!" Otis stated.

"Like hell you do, Otis!" another of the dragoons put in. "That could tell him we ain't fixing to go back to San Patricio."

"They'll do, Sergeant Smith," Ole Devil declared, unaware of the discussion that was taking place among the other party. "Mount up and move out in column of twos."

"Yo!" the newly promoted noncom responded, and gave the necessary orders, reading the unspoken approbation for the way he had acted in his superior's tone and nod of approval.

Instead of accompanying his men as they started to carry out Smith's commands, Ole Devil swung astride but kept his gelding motionless. From this point of vantage, he turned his attention to the dragoons. They all were still clustered around the grave of their deceased, if unlamented, officer. Although a few of them tried to look defiantly at him, not one continued to do so when they found themselves the subject of his Mephistophelian-faced scrutiny.

"I'll leave you to take care of things here, Sergeant Otis," Ole Devil announced, satisfied that there would be no attempt at a last-minute interference. "Adios."

"Adios, Cap'n," the burly noncom replied, stiffening to a brace and delivering the smartest salute he had ever managed.

Riding up the slope after his men, Ole Devil saw that Diamond Hitch Brindley and Tommy were waiting for him on the rim.

"It's allus handy to have a climb like this at the start," the girl commented as the Texian reached her, knowing that he was interested in every aspect of the mule train's operation. "Happen there's anything wrong, it'll show up a whole heap sooner than on level ground."

Ole Devil did not need to have the point clarified. Some horses and, he assumed, mules developed an annoying habit of filling their lungs to capacity, which caused the body to expand, when being saddled. The subsequent expulsion of the air allowed the girths, bellyband, and latigo strap to become slack. Of course, with packers of the Tejas Indians' caliber, each man knew the habits of the individual members of his string too well to have been tricked by such a basic subterfuge. However, there were other problems that might result from the rig's having been fitted incorrectly. Once the animals were on the move, particularly when climbing or going down a slope, any such deficiencies would soon become obvious.

Before the Texian could comment, he saw a further example of Sergeant Smith's forethought. A number of horses belonging to the Arizona Hopi Activos Regiment, including several excellent mounts from the officers who had been killed, had been collected after the battle. Along with the reserve animals of Company C and the dragoons, they had been grazing on top of the rim under the care of three cavalrymen. Without needing instructions from his superior, the noncom had caused the dragoons' horses to be cut out of the remuda[1] and they were being driven to their owners. As the mule train had already gone by, the remainder was set into motion to follow them.

Not only had Smith dealt with the matter of the remuda—and removed a possible cause for the dragoons to harbor resentment—but also, to Ole Devil's satisfaction, he could find no fault in the way that the positioning of the escort had been arranged. Five men were going out on each flank, but all the remainder were staying behind the remuda.

"I had a word with Tom Wolf afore he lit out for San Felipe, Cap'n," the noncom explained on reporting to Ole Devil. "He's sent two of his boys on ahead and one out beyond our flank riders. But I figured, what with that bunch back there"—he gestured with a thumb toward the rim—"and all, we'd best have a good strong rear guard."

"I agree, Sergeant," the Texian answered, well pleased with his subordinate's shrewd assessment of the situation's needs. "If there should be any trouble, it's most likely to come from behind."

Satisfied that all was under control, needing no further attention or action on his part, Ole Devil settled down to continue his study of the art of handling a large packtrain.

With each flank party varying their distance so that they were always just within sight and a Tejas scout farther off beyond them, the concourse of animals and riders headed north. Under the ever-watchful eyes of the packers, but picking their own routes along the line of march instead of being made to travel one behind another, the mules ambled at a steady pace that covered five to six miles an hour. There was, Ole Devil observed, little confusion and no jostling or pushing among them. Like all animals with well-developed herd-

1. Remuda: from the Spanish word meaning "replacement" which was adopted by the Texians to describe a collection of spare mounts herded together and not at the time under saddle. Also occasionally called a *remotha*, pronounced "remootha," a corruption of the Spanish word for *remount, remonta*. In later years cowhands in the Northwest used the terms *cavvy* or *saddle band*.

living instincts, they had acquired a hierarchy in which each knew and, unless capable of changing it by bluff or physical means, was kept in its place. For all their individual desire to get as close as possible to the bell mare, only the most dominant of them could do so. Those lower down the social scale had learned by painful experience that it did not pay to try to usurp the places of their betters.

Apart from the climb out of Santa Cristóbal Bay, the first few hours of the journey were spent traversing terrain which allowed easy travel and presented no problems. It was fairly open, if rolling, range with no steep slopes or other obstacles to be negotiated. There were a few streams, but none was more than twenty feet wide or deeper than about a foot. In addition, there was plenty of rich and nutritious grazing, of which, like the water, the mules availed themselves. They snatched up mouthfuls of liquid or the hock-deep grass while on the move and without causing delays.

With each passing mile, Ole Devil grew more impressed by the packers' skill at attending to their duties. They were constantly on the alert, watching their charges and ready to cope with any emergency. On the few occasions when a load needed adjusting for any reason, the animal would be led clear of its companions, the blindfold affixed, and the correction carried out without hindrance to the rest.

Ole Devil could soon see why Di had been so confident that they could make any pursuit a long process. What was more, he realized that a pack mule might be at a disadvantage in the earlier stages of a journey if they started together, but—as Di had claimed—by the time thirty miles were covered, it would be pushing any horse. The girl also explained that mules had great endurance, tolerated thirst well, could put up with changes in food and climate, and were not fastidious regarding the former. So, on a march of from seventy-five to a hundred miles—particularly in barren and rugged country—they could have even the best of horses at their mercy. In addition, as he was seeing, when cared for by attendants who understood them and gave them proper handling, they were not troublesome, being easy to look after and keep in condition. A further good quality was their ability, resulting from a keen sense of smell, to keep together when on the move through the night. Against that, they had a resentment of violence. This, along with a shyness toward strangers and being touchy about the head and ears, could make them free kickers and had done much to give them their reputation for truculence.

Toward noon, as Di, Ole Devil, and Tommy were preceding the rest of the party in the ascent of a gentle incline, the first serious obstacle came into view from its top.

"I'm damned if I can make out where the son of a bitch ends," the girl told her companions, standing in her stirrups and gazing from under her right hand at the distant woodland across their proposed line of march. "If I could and it wasn't too far, I'd say we start to go so's we'd swing around. Trouble being, we might have to yet, comes to that."

"Ancient and wise Nipponese saying, which I've just made up," Tommy remarked, from his place at Di's right. Ignoring her well-simulated moan of anguish, he went on. "When a person is in doubt, he should always look carefully before making up his mind how to act. That way he will know before it's too late that he's not doing the wrong thing."

"Well, dog my cats from now to then and back!" the girl said, slapping a hand on her thigh and turning an expression of wonderment to the Texian. "*I'd* never've thought of *that.*"

"Which is why humble and unworthy self mentioned it," the little Oriental pointed out imperturbably.

"Well, I'll tell you something, Tommy," Ole Devil drawled, giving the girl no chance to get another word in. "You just beat *me* to suggesting it."

"I'll be eternally damned if one of 'em's not's bad's the other!" Di almost wailed, turning her face upward as if in search of strength and guidance from the heavens. Then she snapped her fingers as if a thought had struck her and continued. "Hey, though, I've just now had an idea—"

"I *knew* it would have to happen one day," Ole Devil declared. "Why don't we push on ahead and find out if we can take the mules through?"

"That's what I was aiming to say," Di protested indignantly. "How'd you get to figuring it out?"

"Just fortunate, I reckon," Ole Devil replied.

"I suppose one or the other of you varmints had to get lucky and say something right sometime." The girl sniffed. "Let's go."

Without allowing either of her companions an opportunity to reply or bothering to tell Joe Galton—who had almost caught up with them—what she was doing, Di urged her mount to increase its speed. She knew that the *cargador* was aware of the need to examine the woodland and would not require an explanation. Tall, well built, in his early twenties, with red hair and a ruggedly good-looking face, the buckskin-clad Galton was Ewart Brindley's adopted son and, like her, fully conversant with every aspect of their family's business.

Holding their horses to a fast trot, the girl, the Texian, and the little Oriental were soon approaching the two Tejas forward scouts, who had halted at the edge of the trees. The woodland stretched as far as they could see in either direction and, if it should prove unsuitable for the mules to pass through, would involve them in a lengthy and time-consuming detour.

"Mannen's detail went in," Ole Devil remarked, indicating the tracks left by his cousin's party, which they had been following since leaving the bay. He swung a challenging glare in Di's direction. "But before *anybody* tells me, I know that they only had horses and not mules carrying packs."

"Now me, I've given up on trying to tell either of you smarty britches anything," the girl declared in tones of deepest disgust, studying the trees. "Anyways, unless it gets thicker further in, we'll not have any trouble getting through."

Joined by the scouts, the trio rode onward, still following the route taken by Mannen Blaze and his detail. At first there were massive live oaks, pecans, black walnuts, and eastern cottonwoods, interspersed, although not too thickly, with a variety of bushes and Carolina buckthorn shrubs, through which wound paths made by wild animals or the semidomesticated longhorn cattle that eventually became a major fact in the economy of Texas. However, after having advanced for about three-quarters of a mile, they came across box elders, silver maples, and American hornbeams[2] which warned them what to expect. So they were not surprised when they emerged from the trees to find themselves looking across about fifty yards of open ground at a river. While it was narrow, compared with the San Bernard, which they would have to cross on their way to Washington-on-the-Brazos, it was considerably wider than any of the streams they had already come over that day.

"Afore I get told, I know *they* went over here," Di announced, indicating the tracks of the previous party and riding forward to scan the muddy water in a futile attempt to discover what lay beneath the surface. "Only, that don't mean the mules can tote packs across. It looks like it might be all right, but I suppose I'll be the one who has to make sure."

"I've always been taught it's polite to let a lady go first," Ole Devil replied, but he knew that the girl was far better qualified than himself to make the decision.

Having told the scouts in their own language—which she spoke fluently—to go along the banks and see if there was anywhere more suitable for a crossing, Di rode into the water. For all her levity when addressing Ole Devil, she was in deadly earnest as she pressed onward. She watched the level of the water as it crept higher and reached the tapaderos[3] of

2. American hornbeam: *Carpinus caroliniana*, a small tree with birchlike leaves, also known as the blue or water beech.
3. Tapadero: in speech usually shortened to *taps*, a wedge-shaped piece of leather covering the stirrup at the front and sides, but open at the rear. Made from heavy cowhide, often carved decoratively, it is used to protect the rider's feet.

her stirrups so she was compelled to raise her feet to avoid it. Much to her relief, it did not get much deeper. What was more, the current was not too fast, and there was a bed of firm gravel with no rocks protruding from it.

However, the girl did not restrict herself to making a single crossing. Instead, she waded back and forth on different lines until she had covered an area about fifty yards in width. Satisfied with the results of her examination, she waved for Ole Devil and Tommy to join her. When they had done so, the trio continued until the woodland ended. If anything, the terrain was slightly better—although forward visibility was still restricted—on the western bank.

"We can get through all right," Di declared. "Let's go back and do it."

Retracing the route they had taken while conducting their examination, the trio did not wait for the scouts to return and report. On reaching the point at which they had entered the woodland, they found that the leaders of the mule train were about a hundred yards away. Di signaled with a beckoning motion, and Galton kept coming.

"We've been through better places, Joe," the girl stated. "And worse."

"Likely," replied the *cargador*, who had a reputation for never using two words when one would suffice.

Moving aside, while Di accompanied Galton, Ole Devil and Tommy watched the mules going by. After about half of them had passed, Prays Loudly, Sometimes came along. Wanting to see what kinds of problems might be met under such conditions, the Texian rode alongside the packer.

Much to Ole Devil's surprise, although Prays Loudly, Sometimes and his companions were clearly exercising extra vigilance, the passage through the trees was being accomplished without any great difficulty. Wending their individual ways along, the mules displayed an awareness of where they could or could not go. They never tried to pass through a gap that was too narrow for themselves and their burdens.

Remembering some of the comments he had heard Di

make, the Texian stayed with the packer for only half a mile. Then he went forward to catch up with her and Galton. By the time he reached them, they were on the banks of the river, and he knew that he was going to witness another important part of a mule train's activities.

The first thing to strike Ole Devil's notice was that the four leading packers had already joined the girl and the *cargador*. Leading the bell mare into the water, Galton started to cross. Looking back, he found that the foremost mules were hesitating, and leaning over, he took hold of the leather collar to give the bell a vigorous shake. After a moment the sound and a reluctance to be parted from the mare produced the desired effect without the need for action on the part of Di and the packers.

As the animals entered the water, the packers accompanied them. More of the Tejas came up, following their companions. However, none of them went straight to the other side. Ole Devil could understand why they halted to form a double line through which their charges were passing. If one of the heavily loaded mules should stumble and go down, the weight of its pack would prevent it from rising. Unless it was helped quickly, it would drown. What was more, its struggles might frighten the others and make them refuse to go on.

No such tragedy occurred, and the crossing went by uneventfully. Before going over himself, Ole Devil waited for the remuda and the rear guard to pass. Wisely, since the horses lacked the mules' incentive to stick together, Sergeant Smith had reinforced their herders on reaching the woodland. The noncom also told him that there was no sign of anybody following them, nor had the flank parties reported anything of interest.

With the woodland behind them, Di called a halt. Once again, Ole Devil became aware of the apparent intelligence of what he had previously regarded as stubborn and somewhat stupid animals. Each mule stood patiently until its packer could fasten on its blindfold, remove its burden, and examine its back and hooves. Not until that had been done and its eyes uncovered did it attempt first to enjoy a good roll and then start to graze. In addition to the grass it consumed, each was given a feed of grain from the packs carried by the reserve mules.

"You know something, Di?" Ole Devil remarked as he and the girl were strolling around, watching the work being carried out. "I've been wrong about mules. They're smarter than I realized."

"Figuring 'em's being stupid's a mistake most folks's haven't been around 'em much make," Di replied. "Mules're as smart and in some ways even smarter'n hosses. All you have to do is treat 'em right and train 'em properly."

"There's a rider coming, Cap'n Hardin!" Smith called, before the discussion could be continued. "Can't make out who it is yet, but he's waving."

"It must be to us," Di guessed. "If he wasn't somebody's they figured was all right, the scouts would've let us know afore now."

Putting the matter of the mules from his mind temporarily, Ole Devil gazed in the direction indicated by the noncom. He watched the horseman coming toward them at a gallop. Although he, too, failed to make an identification at first, he was in agreement with the girl's assumption. It proved to be correct. In a short while the rider was close enough to be recognized.

"It's young Sammy Cope, Cap'n," Smith decided, having joined his superior and Di so as to be ready if any action had to be taken. "Mr. Blaze must've sent him back to report, unless something's wrong."

A few seconds later they all could tell that the sergeant's doubts were unfounded. Although showing signs of having ridden a long distance at speed, the lanky young enlisted man displayed nothing but a cheerful satisfaction at having reached his destination.

"Come and walk his horse until it cools down, one of you men!" Ole Devil called, as the newcomer brought his lathered mount to a halt and dismounted.

"*Gracias,* Cap'n," Cope said gratefully, handing the reins to the man who hurried forward. "He's been running plenty. Mr. Blaze told me to get back here and meet you's fast's I could, 'n' that's what I've done."

"Is everything all right with him?" Ole Devil asked.

"Sure is, Cap'n," Cope replied, and looked at the girl. "Your grandpappy's doing right well, Di. He was cussing fit to bust and said I should tell you that he'll take a switch to your hide happen you lose any of them knob-heads."

"Is the ferry at Hickert's Landing still in use?" Ole Devil inquired, guessing why his cousin had sent the man.

"Yes, sir, Cap'n," Cope answered.

"I told youse ole Mose Hickert 'n' his boys wouldn't've pulled out," Di put in, but there was relief in her voice.

The girl's emotion did not entirely stem from learning that her grandfather was making the far from comfortable trip with no worsening of his condition. She had known that they were faced with crossing the San Bernard River. It would be a different, much more difficult proposition from the one they had forded in the woodland unless the services of the ferry at Hickert's Landing were still available. While mules were excellent swimmers, they could not do so when they were carrying such heavy weights. Nor was there anywhere along the San Bernard that was sufficiently shallow at this time of the year for them to be able to wade across. They could ride on the ferry, having been trained to do so. However, if it had gone, Di's men would have to make rafts and float the consignment over, allowing the unburdened animals to swim without impediment.

"Mr. Blaze said for me to tell you he's left half of our fellers at the landing, Cap'n," Cope went on. "He figured it'd be best in case them San Felipe varmints come around with notions of making fuss for you there."

"Good for ole Mannen," Di said, darting a mischievous grin at the satanic-looking Texian. She was delighted to hear they had reinforcements waiting, even if it was only twelve men, but she was unable to resist the temptation to strike back at her occasional tormentor. "It's lucky there's *one* right smart *hombre* in your family, Devil."

"Hey!" Cope almost yelped, having been looking around, before his superior could think up a suitable reply. "Where at's all them dragoons?"

"They're pulled out 'n' gone home," Di replied.

"They won't be no loss, wasn't one of 'em worth a cuss any way at all," Cope declared, displaying no more concern than the other members of his company had over the departure of the dragoons. "You want for me to head back after Mr. Blaze, Cap'n."

"No," Ole Devil decided. "You can stay with us from here on. Go grab something to eat, then pick yourself a fresh horse from the remuda."

"It's about time things started to go smoother for us," Di commented as the enlisted man ambled away. "You could head for San Patricio now if you're so minded."

"I've considered it," Ole Devil admitted, "but I think I can go easier in my mind after I've seen you safe across the San Bernard."

Although the Texian and the girl did not realize it, he had made what was to prove a most fortunate decision.

8

WE'LL HAVE TO FIND OUT
THE HARD WAY

"What do you think, Tommy?" Ole Devil Hardin inquired as bringing their four horses to a halt while still partially concealed among the trees, he and the little Oriental studied the opposite bank of the small river they had forded about twenty-four hours earlier. "Did I see something over there?"

The crossing of the San Bernard River had been accomplished, as the result of the help given willingly by the Hickert family, without any great difficulty. However, darkness had fallen before the consignment and everybody concerned in its protection were on the eastern shore. So, eager as he was to set off on the reconnaissance mission, Ole Devil had realized that Diamond Hitch Brindley was making her usual good sense when she had suggested he and Tommy Okasi take a night's rest before leaving. They were going to need all their wits about them, which would not be the case if they were tired. Nor would they be able to sleep with such a measure of safety once they had parted company from their companions.

While Ole Devil and Tommy were returning to the south, the remainder of the party was to make its way to the Brazos

River. Once there, despite its making a large curve to the
east above the lower reaches' most westerly bend, they
would stay on the banks instead of following Mannen Blaze
and the injured men who had gone straight overland to
Thompson's Ferry. When discussing the proposed route with
Di and Joe Galton, Ole Devil had envisaged one difficulty
which might arise. The girl had assured him that with the
mules she was employing, it would not present any problem,
and he had bowed to her superior knowledge in such matters. One further point had been settled. Although the other
citizens of Hickert's Landing had already fled, the family was
remaining to continue operating the ferry until there was
danger from the approaching Mexican forces.

Being aware of the need to travel fast, Ole Devil and the
little Oriental had made careful preparations. To conserve
their personal mounts, all of which had been worked very
hard over the past few days, they had selected the best two of
the dead Mexican officers' horses to ride during the earlier
stages of the journey. The animals' burdens had been reduced to the bare necessities: a telescope; arms and a small
supply of ammunition; cloak coats, but neither a change of
clothing nor blankets; some jerky and pemmican—easily
transported and nutritious—for food. Superbly mounted and
excellent riders, they were capable of covering at least fifty
miles a day. However, once they were drawing near to their
destination, they would be compelled to take precautions
which would require a reduction of their speed. So they intended to make the best possible time before they were required to go more slowly.

For all the urgency of their mission and in spite of believing they would be unlikely to come into contact with any of
the enemy before the following day at the earliest, the Texian
and his companion were too experienced campaigners to
take any unnecessary chances. Instead of sticking to the trail
which they had traversed with the mule train, they had made
their way out of sight and parallel to it. However, on reaching the area of thick woodland, they had accepted that they

would have to make use of the same ford at which they had crossed the small river. According to the flanking parties, this was the only point at which they could go over without considerable effort and difficulty.

As he and Tommy were approaching the ford, Ole Devil thought that he detected something moving among the undergrowth on the other side. Although he had received only a very brief glimpse and it was not repeated, they had come to a halt while still in at least partial concealment. There was close to fifty yards of completely open ground on either side of the river, and they wanted to make sure they could cross it in safety.

"I can't see anything," the little Oriental answered, having completed his scrutiny. "But there are many places for anybody who wants to be able to hide."

"That's for sure," Ole Devil declared, and began to unfasten the reins of his reserve mount from the saddle horn of the horse he was sitting. "So it looks as if we'll have to find out the hard way. I'll go first."

"Let me get ready, just in case," Tommy requested, swinging to the ground.

While he had been alert and watchful, the little Oriental was not holding his bow. Because its length would have made it too unwieldy to be used with any great effect in the woodland, he had preferred to leave his hands free for manipulating his sword. So the bow was hanging unstrung on the loops of his saddle's skirts, and the quiver of arrows was suspended from the horn instead of across his shoulders. However, the circumstances might have changed, and if he needed to support his employer, archery would provide him with the best means of doing so.

"Very old and wise Louisiana saying, which *I've* just made up," Ole Devil drawled, delighted at having an opportunity to do so. "A man should always be ready; then he wouldn't have to get ready."

Unlike his companion, who looked pained at the comment, the young Texian was already armed in a suitable manner to cope with whatever emergency should arise. With an overall length of 58⅞ inches, the weapon resting across the crook of his left elbow had a similar general appearance to that of a so-called Kentucky[1] rifle. A closer examination would have disclosed that it was a far more sophisticated device. It was, in fact, an invention of the Mormon gunsmith Jonathan Browning, designed to meet the requirement for a firearm which could discharge several shots in succession and without the need for each to be loaded individually.[2] So the Browning slide repeating rifle[3] possessed qualities which Ole Devil had considered more than compensated for the

1. The majority of what have come to be known as Kentucky rifles were manufactured in Pennsylvania.
2. For the benefit of those who have not read *Young Ole Devil, Ole Devil and the Caplocks,* or *Get Urrea,* the Browning slide repeating rifle was one of the earliest successful American-designed multiple-firing weapons. The slide magazine—generally with a capacity of five shots, although greater numbers could be had if requested—was a rectangular iron bar, drilled to take percussion caps and the main firing charge, which passed through an aperture at the rifle's breech. When operated by the thumb, a lever at the right side of the frame moved each successive chamber into position and cammed the slide forward to form a gastight connection against the bore. Because of its proximity to the front of the trigger guard, the underhammer could easily be cocked by the right forefinger without the shooter's taking the rifle's butt from the shoulder.
    Despite the difficulty of transporting it for any length of time with the magazine in position, the rifle was simple in operation and capable of a continuous fire unequaled by any other firearm available in 1836. However, during the period of its manufacture, between 1834 and 1842, Browning lacked the facilities for large-scale manufacture. He would have been able to do so in later years, but the development of self-contained metal-cased cartridges and more compact, if less simple, weapons had rendered it obsolete.
3. While engaged in manufacturing the slide repeating rifle, Jonathan Browning, q.v., also developed a rifle which could be fired six times in succession. The charges were held in a cylinder, but there was no mechanism, and it had to be rotated manually after each shot. While the same caliber—roughly .45—and almost ten inches shorter, it was more bulky and weighed twelve pounds two ounces as opposed to the slide repeating rifle's nine pounds fourteen ounces. It was not offered for sale until Browning had settled at Council Bluffs, Utah, in 1852. However, by that

inconvenience of carrying it by hand, as opposed to in the leather boot—an innovation of a young saddler, Joe Gaylin, who in later years attained considerable acclaim as a maker of superlative gun belts—attached to the left side of his saddle, while traveling through such difficult terrain.

"If you're going to start making up ancient and wise sayings," Tommy declared as he tied the reins of his borrowed horse to a bush and, lifting free the quiver, slung it across his shoulder, "I think I'll face the shogun's wrath and go home."

The bow stave which the little Oriental drew from its loops on the skirt of his saddle was constructed in the classical Japanese fashion. It was built of three strips of bamboo, sheathed on two sides by mulberry wood, forming a core which was encased by two further lengths of bamboo and pasted with fish glue, the whole being painted with lacquer. Laminating the bamboo and the softer, more pliable mulberry wood achieved a greater strength and flexibility than if a "self" bow were manufactured from either material.

Taking the bow's coiled *tsuru* hemp string from a pocket of his tunic, Tommy shook it straight. Then he slipped the appropriate loop into the *urahazu* upper nock groove of the stave. Holding the lower end of the *tsuru* between his teeth, he wedged the top of the bow under a branch of the nearest tree and supported the bottom with his right hand against the top of his slightly bent left leg. Grasping the *nigiri* handle with his left hand and pushing at it, he flexed the bow. Removing the *tsuru* from his teeth with his right thumb and forefinger, he gave it the traditional three outward twists before applying the second loop to the *motohazu* bottom nock. Although he did not bother to check, as the bow was properly strung, the distance between the handle and the *nakishikake* nocking binding of the *tsuru* could have been spanned by his fist with its thumb extended and was approximately the same width as that between his cheekbones.

time, it, too, had become redundant as the result of the ever-increasing availability of Samuel Colt's mechanically superior rifles and revolvers.

Having completed his preparations, Tommy removed the top of the bow from beneath the branch and took two arrows from the quiver with his right hand. Although he had made them since his arrival in Texas, he had used the methods learned in his homeland.[4] Holding one by its head, so that the shaft was pointing to his rear, he nocked the other to the *nakishikake*. Then, adopting a position of readiness which was somewhat different from that of an Occidental archer,[5] he gave a low, sibilant hiss which drew Ole Devil's attention from the other side of the river, then nodded.

While the little Oriental had been making ready to cover him if the need should arise, the Texian had tried without avail to locate any sign of danger. Having failed to do so, he allowed his dun's split-ended reins to fall free, thus ground hitching it. Easing down the rifle's underhammer to full cock, he set the Mexican's bay between his legs moving at a walk. On leaving the shelter of the trees, he continued to keep the terrain ahead under constant observation.

Still without seeing anything to disturb him, the Texian guided his mount into the river. As it advanced, he removed his feet from the stirrups and raised his legs to avoid the water which was soon lapping at the horse's belly. If there had been the slightest suggestion that enemies were lurking in concealment, he would not have acted in such a manner. Believing that there was no cause for alarm and knowing he had neither the time nor the means to dry his footwear, he wanted to save it from getting wet.

"Look out down there!" yelled a voice from among the

4. The traditional Japanese arrow was made from *mashino-dake*, a very straight, hard, and thin species of bamboo. After being cut in the winter, the bamboo was left to dry out of doors until spring. Having been further dried and hardened by being placed close to a fire, the joints were carefully smoothed down. When the shaft had been polished with emery powder and water, it was once more exposed to the fire. Finally, it was fletched with three feathers from a hawk, falcon, or eagle and had its metal arrowhead and nock affixed.
5. See footnote 11 on page 9.

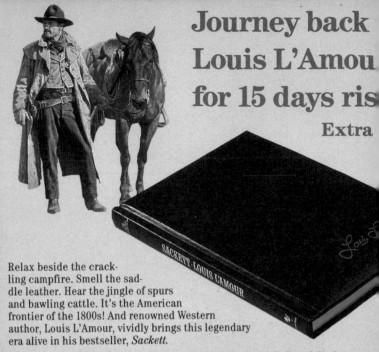

Journey back
Louis L'Amou
for 15 days ris
Extra

Relax beside the crackling campfire. Smell the saddle leather. Hear the jingle of spurs and bawling cattle. It's the American frontier of the 1800s! And renowned Western author, Louis L'Amour, vividly brings this legendary era alive in his bestseller, *Sackett*.

Ride into the high country with young Tell Sackett. Follow him into a hidden canyon where he discovers a lost gold mine. It's going to be his secret stake. But the secret doesn't last for long. When Tell and the beautiful Kerry Ange return to the mine, they're trapped by a lawless gang of desperadoes who aim to take the gold and leave no witnesses. If you love action-packed adventure . . .

. . . if the romance of the frontier stirs you . . . if stories that spring from real life appeal to you—you will love *Sackett*. It's a fabulous read and an ideal introduction to the best-selling novels in *The Louis L'Amour Collection!* See for yourself. Preview *Sackett* in a handsomely crafted hardcover Collector's Edition at your leisure for 15 days risk-free.

SAVE OVER HALF OFF!

If you enjoy *Sackett* as much as I know you will and decide to keep it, simply honor our invoice for only $4.95—*A SAVINGS OF OVER HALF OFF* the current low regular rate of $11.95—plus shipping and handling, and sales tax in NY and Canada, as your introduction to *The Collection* under the terms on the post card at the right.

As soon as we hear from you, your full-color Louis L'Amour Wall Calendar will be on its way—yours to keep absolutely *FREE*. You can't miss! Act now to claim your *FREE GIFT* and *RISK-FREE PREVIEW*!

e Old West with

ompelling novel, *Sackett*,
ee!

l: You may keep *Sackett* for only $4.95!*

Detach and mail this postpaid card to preview *Sackett* for 15 days risk-free and to claim your Free Gift!

RISK-FREE TRIAL CERTIFICATE
FREE GIFT!   FREE PREVIEW!

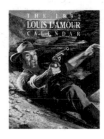 

SAVE OVER HALF OFF!

☐ YES. Send my free Louis L'Amour Wall Calendar and my hardbound Collector's Edition of *Sackett* for a 15-day risk-free preview. If I keep it, I'll honor your invoice for only $4.95—a SAVINGS OF OVER HALF OFF the current low regular rate of $11.95—plus shipping and handling, and sales tax in NY and Canada. Then I'll continue receiving additional selections about once a month at the regular rate on the same 15-day risk-free trial basis. There's no minimum number of books I must buy, and I may cancel at any time. The Calendar is mine to keep no matter what I decide.   IL6   41400

Name	(please print)

Address		Apt.

City	State	Zip

SEND NO MONEY NOW

In Addition to the Free Louis L'Amour Calendar

. . . your risk-free preview volume of *Sackett* will introduce you to these outstanding qualities of the bookbinder's art—

- Each volume is bound in rich, rugged sierra-brown simulated leather.

- The bindings are sewn, not just glued, to last a lifetime. And the pages are printed on high-quality paper that is acid-free and will not yellow with age.

- The title and Louis L'Amour's signature are golden embossed on the spine and front cover of each volume.

foliage of a large silver maple tree as Ole Devil was about three-quarters of the way across and contemplating returning his feet to the stirrups. "Indians!"

Even as the warning was given, a young Hopi brave lunged out of the undergrowth some thirty yards to the right of the speaker. Leaping forward, he raised and propelled his curved throwing stick through the air. What was more, it had left his hand before the words could affect his aim.

Just after the weapon had left the brave's hand, three somewhat older warriors followed him into the open ground. One held a short wooden "self" bow with an arrow nocked to its string but not yet drawn. The second grasped a flintlock rifle, and the last was carrying a lance. While his companions followed the first of their number to appear, the man with the firearm turned toward the tree from which the warning had originated. For all that it had been in English, he guessed its meaning and knew it must have been uttered by an enemy. Peering at the thick canopy of leaves that covered the branches as he advanced, he came to a halt before he had taken half a dozen steps. Snapping the rifle's butt to his shoulder, he lined the barrel upward.

Watching the missile as it was approaching, Ole Devil could tell that it was flying straight toward him and not so as to pass by him. Nor did he underestimate the danger it presented. In fact, he realized that it could prove even more effective than an arrow or a bullet under the circumstances.[6] Spinning toward him at chest height and parallel to the ground, the three-foot-long throwing stick—made from a

6. The throwing stick of the Hopi and related tribes of North American Indians is a similar device to the war and hunting boomerangs of the Australian aborigines, but is neither designed nor expected to return to the thrower if it should miss its target. This does not make it any less lethal as a weapon. American author Daniel Mannix described in Chapter 7, "The Boomerang, the Stick That Kills," of his book *A Sporting Chance* —which covers the subject thoroughly, along with other unusual methods of hunting—how he has thrown one a distance of 540 feet and still it retained sufficient momentum to crack an inch-thick branch of a tree.

carefully selected and shaped branch of a Gambel oak tree (*Quercus gambelii*)—stood far less chance of missing than either of the comparatively narrow missiles and was capable of striking even harder.

Although neither he nor Tommy had come into contact with throwing sticks before their meeting with the Hopis, Ole Devil was all too aware of his peril. Having an affinity for primitive weapons, the little Oriental had been able to assess the device's potential. What was more, while waiting for the mule train to move out of Santa Cristóbal Bay, they had taken an opportunity to experiment and confirm his conclusions.

In spite of Ole Devil's left hand shaking his mount's one-piece Mexican pattern reins from between his second and third fingers, so that they fell onto the saddle horn, he knew that trying to raise the rifle and shoot would avail him nothing. He might kill the young brave, but the weapon had already been thrown at him. Nor, from what he had seen and Tommy had told him, would trying to deflect the missile serve his purpose any better. On coming into contact with the Browning's barrel, even if no other damage was inflicted, the stick would not be halted. It would either knock the rifle from his grasp or, failing that, spin around the barrel and retain sufficient impetus to reach and strike him with considerable force.

Accepting that there was only one course left open to him, the Texian took it. Grasping the rifle firmly with both hands, he quit the horse's back. There was no time for him to try to throw a leg forward and jump clear in the hope of landing on his feet. Instead, he toppled sideways to the left out of the saddle. Even as he was going down, he heard the hissing of the throwing stick as it twirled rapidly by not a foot above him. Then, as he plunged into the river, he thrust up the rifle in an attempt to prevent it from accompanying him below the surface.

Annoyance filled the young Hopi as he saw that he had missed his target. The missile was an old favorite which could be counted upon always to fly in the same fashion when thrown correctly, and he might not be able to find it in the woods across the river. However, he derived consolation from the thought that he could obtain some even more satisfactory and modern weapons from the Texian. As the first to count coup,[7] he would be entitled to the pick of the dismounted victim's property. So, snatching the knife from its sheath on his belt, he continued to run toward the water's edge.

Having seen Ole Devil evade the throwing stick, Tommy returned his attention to the Indians. Commencing his draw, he knew that he must decide—and very quickly—which of the braves to aim at.

What was more, the answer must be correct!

For all his comparatively modern weapon, Tommy concluded that the man with the rifle could be ignored. He was concentrating upon whoever had called the warning from among the foliage of the silver maple.

Being closest, the youngest brave was posing the most immediate threat. With that in mind, Tommy selected and started to take aim at him.

The action was not completed!

Slower than the lance carrier, who still ran on, the fourth warrior skidded to a halt. Raising his bow, he began to pull back on the string and sight the arrow. When it was released, it would fly much faster than either of his companions was capable of moving. So, no matter who counted the first coup, the honor of killing the paleface would be his.

As soon as he struck the river's bed, Ole Devil twisted himself upward until he was sitting slightly less than chest deep in the water. Seeing the young brave approaching, with

7. Unlike the Comanches, who allowed only the first arrival to count the coup—which was done by touching preferably a living enemy or a corpse and saying, *"A:he!,"* meaning "I claim it!"—the Hopi and some other tribes permitted the second and third warrior to take lesser shares in the credit.

the lance carrier following about fifteen feet to the rear, he snapped the Browning's butt to his shoulder. Noticing the man with the bow preparing to shoot at him, he guessed at what Tommy was doing and knew that he must handle his nearest attackers himself. So he squinted along the 40 5/16-inch octagonal barrel rather than the V-shaped notch of the rear right.

Although the young Hopi saw he was being covered, he was not especially perturbed. He had never used a firearm but knew enough about the shortcomings of those owned by other members of his nation to feel he was in no danger. What he failed to appreciate was that he did not face a flintlock, the powder in the priming pan of which would almost certainly have been ruined when its owner fell into the river.

The Browning rifle was not impervious to water, but it was less susceptible to its effects than the older type of mechanism. For all that, Ole Devil knew a misfire would put him in a desperate situation. Squeezing the trigger, he felt the hammer being liberated and start to snap upward.

Even as Tommy was altering the alignment of his weapon, a shot crashed from the other side of the river. It was the sharp detonation of a fairly light-caliber handgun, probably a dueling pistol, not the deeper roar of a shoulder arm. Back jerked the head of the brave with the rifle. A blue-rimmed hole appeared in the center of his brow, and the base of his skull burst open as the bullet emerged. Toppling over, he fired his weapon harmlessly into the air, and it fell from his grasp.

Refusing to let himself be distracted by the shooting, Tommy made sure of his aim and loosed the arrow. It flashed across the intervening space, but not quite to the mark at which it had been directed. Going past the youngest brave as he was being struck in the left breast by Ole Devil's bullet, it hit and sliced through the upper limb of the warrior's bow. For all that, the effect of the shot served the little Oriental's purpose. It snatched the ruined weapon from the Hopi's hands before he could release his own shaft. Letting out a startled yelp, he staggered backward.

Sharing the younger brave's summation of the situation, the lance carrier was surprised when Ole Devil's rifle went off. To his annoyance, he saw his stricken companion spin around and, dropping the knife, blunder into his path. Swerving around the falling youngster, he hardly noticed that the bay was startled by the shot and beginning to lope away. He found the behavior of the paleface of greater interest. Not only was he still sitting down, but he made no attempt to take the rifle from his shoulder. Yet its single barrel must now be empty.

Not for the first time Ole Devil's life was depending upon the reliability of Jonathan Browning's inventive genius and skilled craftsmanship. Thrusting down the lever with his thumb, he watched the magazine creeping slowly through the aperture. Nearer rushed the Hopi, his lance held ready for use and savage determination etched in the lines of his face.

9

THEY'RE CLOSER THAN
WE EXPECTED

Even as the Browning slide repeating rifle's magazine halted
and was cammed into position against the barrel's bore, Ole
Devil Hardin's right forefinger reached around the front of
the trigger guard to cock the underhammer. Although he
had been watching the slide to make sure that it was operating correctly, the sound of water splashing warned him that
his assailant was drawing ever closer. Looking up, he found
that the Hopi brave was already lifting back the lance ready
to strike.

On the eastern bank Tommy Okasi had lowered his right
hand and was allowing the second arrow to slide through it
until he could take hold of the nock. He was such a highly
skilled archer that he had no need to look down and made
the movements instinctively. Affixing the slot of the nock on
the *nakashikake*, he rested the shaft in the shallow V formed
by his left thumb and the bow's handle. While doing so, he
continued to keep the other side of the river under observation. In spite of knowing the rifle's potential, he saw enough
to warn him that his employer was still in deadly peril. What
was more, there might not be sufficient time for him to draw

and aim the arrow with the accuracy that was needed if he was to help.

With the hammer at full cock, Ole Devil returned his finger to the Browning's trigger. There was no need for him to bother about making sure of his aim. Dashing onward recklessly, the Hopi was so near that it would be practically impossible to miss. Nor was he showing the slightest alarm over having the rifle directed at him. Clearly he believed that it was empty and that he had nothing to fear.

Pressure on the Browning's trigger set the firing cycle into motion. Much to Ole Devil's relief, he heard the slight pop as the hammer ignited the percussion cap. Even as flame and white powder smoke was erupting from the barrel in the wake of the .45 caliber round soft lead ball, with the lance driving straight at him and almost level with the rifle's muzzle, he tipped himself to the left.

Shock mingled with the agony that came to the Hopi's face as the bullet plowed into the base of his throat and broke his neck. Although he was mortally wounded, his momentum carried him onward, and the lance was still grasped firmly enough in his hand for it to have achieved his purpose.

Ole Devil's hat had slipped sideways when he fell from his horse, being arrested on his right shoulder by its *barbiquejo*, its chin strap. The tip of the lance brushed its brim in passing, and tripping over him, the dying brave plunged face forward into the river.

Watching along the shaft of his arrow, which he had just drawn until it was at its anchor point ready to be aimed, Tommy let out a hiss of relief as he saw it would not be needed to save his employer. So he began to turn it in search of another target and had no trouble in finding one.

Seeing the fates which had overtaken the rest of his companions, the last Hopi brave decided that discretion was the better part of valor. He regarded the loss of his bow with mixed feelings. While he had been deprived of his main weapon, its destruction had also prevented him from being injured. On the other hand, he now had no way of either

killing the Texian in the river or defending himself against
the man on the opposite bank, who was preparing to launch
another arrow at him. Furthermore, his party was on a scouting mission, and he now had something of importance to
report to his superiors.

Even as he was drawing his conclusions, the brave saw that
the means for escape were at hand. Frightened by the shooting, the horse from which the paleface had fallen was approaching. Darting to meet it, the brave heard the whistle of
an arrow passing close behind him. Grabbing the horse's
saddle horn as it went by, he vaulted onto its back. Then,
flattening himself along its neck to offer a smaller target, he
gave a yell that caused the animal to bound forward even
faster.

Muttering imprecations in English, which he had found
offered a more satisfactory breadth than his native tongue
for expressing annoyance and anger, Tommy reached up to
extract another arrow from his quiver. He realized that he
was unlikely to be able to use it but intended to try in the
hope of bringing down the fleeing Indian.

The little Oriental discovered, while nocking the shaft into
position, that whoever was concealed up the silver maple
tree had a similar idea. Either the pistol was double-barreled, or its user had its mate. No matter which, a second
shot—sounding like its predecessor—came from the foliage.
However, the bullet failed to take effect. Before Tommy
could draw and aim the arrow, the brave had passed beyond
his range of vision among the trees.

Watching the departing warrior as he was coming to his
feet and starting to press the Browning's reloading lever, Ole
Devil spat out a few choice Anglo-Saxon obscenities. Not
only was he soaked to the skin, with no dry clothing into
which he could change, but he had lost one of his horses.
There was some slight consolation to be drawn from the
latter. The animal was carrying nothing except its former
owner's saddle and bridle, to which it was accustomed and
which Ole Devil had used rather than replace it with his

second set of Texas-style rigging. Against that small benefit, he would be unable to travel as quickly now that he was reduced to the services of a single mount.

Wading ashore, after having glanced behind him to make sure there was nothing further to be feared from his lance-carrying assailant, Ole Devil saw the deeply cut and indented leaves of the silver maple, their dull yellow winter hue just starting to change to the colors of spring—pale green on the outer surface and whitish on the inner—being agitated. However, remembering how the person hidden by the foliage had acted, he concluded that there was no cause for concern.

A pair of mud-smeared black Hessian boots, with stained white trousers tucked into them, appeared below one of the silver maple's lowest branches. Even as a tall, slim man dressed in the fashion of a professional gambler swung downward, there was a movement in the same clump of bushes on the left of the tree from which Ole Devil had received his first intimation of danger.

"Don't shoot!" the man yelled as the Texian's Browning began to rise, and he dropped to the ground, showing alarm.

The warning had not been necessary. Before the butt of the rifle had reached his shoulder, Ole Devil was able to study the small figure emerging from the bushes. What he had seen was sufficient to tell him that he would not need the weapon. So he did not complete the movement.

Despite all the hair being tucked out of sight beneath the crown of a wide-brimmed hat and having on a dirt-bespattered brown cloak coat over masculine attire, the newcomer was definitely *not* a man.

Although somewhat haggard and showing signs of considerable strain, the young woman's face was exceptionally pretty and struck Ole Devil as familiar. She was walking slowly, showing every evidence of feeling extremely tired. For all that, there was something of what would have been a graceful and even slightly seductive carriage in more favorable conditions. A bell-mouthed blunderbuss was hanging muzzle downward in her right hand.

"It's Captain Hardin, isn't it?" asked the man, striding forward with an attitude of relief. He had a fine-looking double-barreled percussion-fired pistol thrust into the silk sash around his waist, and an *épée-de-combat* hung sheathed on the slings of his belt. "I thought—and hoped—it might be when I saw you crossing the river, sir, but I couldn't be sure."

Even if seeing the young woman had not supplied him with a clue, Ole Devil would have identified the voice before turning toward the speaker. Its tones were resonant and unforgettable, having been trained to reach the farthest seat of the largest theater without artificial aids and allowing every word to be understood by its occupant.

Clearly in the peak of physical condition, despite having reached his middle forties, the man was impressively handsome. His normally immaculate shoulder-long black hair, which had no covering and was uncombed and unkempt, was still luxuriant and had no traces of gray. Like the young woman, he was showing signs of considerable exertion and much hard traveling. All in all, he was looking far less debonair, elegant, and composed than during his previous meetings with the Texian.

"It is," Ole Devil admitted, somewhat coldly, lowering the Browning and returning its underhammer to the position of safety at half cock.

"Et tu, Brute?"[1] The man sighed, his welcoming smile wavering. Then he shrugged his shoulders and went on half to himself. "I suppose it's only to be unexpected, though hard."

Considering that his life had been saved by the speaker's

---

1. *"Et tu, Brute?,"* "And you also, Brutus?": said to have been Gaius Julius Caesar's reproachful dying comment on discovering that his friend Marcus Junius Brutus was one of the assassins who had attacked him at the foot of Pompey's statue in the Senate Building, Rome, on the fifteenth, "The Ides" of March, 44 B.C., and quoted by the English playwright William Shakespeare (1564–1616) in Act III, Scene One of *Julius Caesar.*

timely warning, the young Texian was behaving in a far less cordial fashion than most people would have expected of him. However, while he was grateful, circumstances had caused him to have misgivings where his savior was concerned.

Prior to his having left the United States, Mangrove Hallistead had appeared with great success at every major theater in that country. Such were his fame, popularity, and general behavior that in spite of the normally marked reluctance shown by many wealthy southern families toward accepting members of the theatrical profession as social equals, he had gained access to the homes of almost every influential Texian family—the majority of whom had their origins south of the Mason-Dixon line[2]—since arriving in Texas.

Ole Devil had met Hallistead on a few occasions and, being of a tolerant nature, had had no scruples in accepting him as a social equal. He had found the entertainer to be well educated, cultured, intelligent, well informed about current events and a gentleman even by the exacting southern interpretation of the word. They had never been more than acquaintances. So although he had wondered why such an obviously talented person—to whom not even the slightest taint of a public scandal had attached itself—should have given up a successful and profitable career to make a home in Texas, convention would not allow him to satisfy his curiosity.

The cause of the young Texian's apparent ingratitude had arisen a few months earlier. After having seemed to be a supporter of Major General Samuel Houston's policies, the

2. Mason-Dixon line, sometimes called the Mason-Dixie line: the boundary between Pennsylvania and Maryland, as surveyed from 1763 to 1767 by the Englishmen Charles Mason and Jeremiah Dixon, which came to be regarded as the dividing line between the southern "slave" and the northern "free" states of America.

entertainer had been one of the first to go and join Colonel Frank W. Johnson at San Patricio.

"My thanks for your warning, sir," Ole Devil said stiffly, puzzled by the other's comment and suspecting that it had implied he was behaving in a churlish manner unbecoming a gentleman.

"I would have called out sooner, but I thought you to be aware of the Indians' presence and, somewhat ill-advisedly in my opinion, were acting as a decoy to lure them into exposing themselves," Hallistead explained, his speech returning to the flamboyance gained in a lifetime on the stage. "And I must tender a further apology for not being able to send an earlier warning. Although, from all I've seen, you managed very well without it."

"I don't understand," Ole Devil stated, and glanced over his shoulder to find that Tommy, riding with feet raised as he had done, was bringing all the horses across the river.

"Manny!" the young woman put in, preventing the conversation from continuing. Her voice had a melodious southern drawl but was also pitched so that it could carry around the auditorium of a large theater. "Mist— Captain Hardin's soaked through to the skin. Surely you-all can let him change into something dry before you start asking questions?"

"Egad, my dove, I concur," Hallistead replied, giving a courtly bow to his wife. "However, the proximity of these noble aborigines"—he gestured toward the nearest of the Hopi Indians' bodies—"presupposes that they have confederates in the offing. I may be reaching an erroneous conclusion, Captain Hardin, but I assume that they are merely a marauding band of indigenous natives and not a portion of the Mexican Army."

"They're members of the Arizona Hopi Activos Regiment, Mr. Hallistead," Ole Devil corrected. "Forward scouts, most likely. We've had trouble with them before, but I thought the main body was at least two days' ride away. If those four mean what I suspect, they're closer than we thought."

"I can't claim that I was aware that they formed part of the force—" the entertainer began.

"Now, Manny!" Corrinne Hallistead interrupted, indignantly stamping a dainty—despite being encased in an unfeminine boot—right foot and looking the satanic-featured young Texian over from head to toe. "Why, the poor captain's just running with water and like to catch a mortal chill. Surely you can let him change into something dry before you go on with your talk?"

"A most level-headed suggestion, as always, light of my very existence," Hallistead conceded, reaching out to take the woman's left hand and kiss it. Then he glanced to where Tommy was dismounting and, returning his gaze to Ole Devil, went on. "Your worthy Oriental factotum has arrived, sir. I trust that you have the vestments suitable for your needs?"

"I haven't," the Texian admitted wryly, knowing that even though the situation might have changed so that he could not continue with his present assignment, he was still faced with a long ride in wet clothing.

"I suspected as much from the paucity of impedimenta attached to your saddles," Hallistead admitted. "Being aware that you are possessed of a strong sense of duty, sir, I can only conclude that you have heard of the happenings at San Patricio, and having seen the consignment of caplocks well on their way to safety, you are returning hotfoot to ascertain—"

"Manny!" Corrinne put in, and her tone took on a sharper, more demanding note.

"Of course, my love," the entertainer answered soothingly. "I'm afraid that I can't help you in the matter of alternative raiment, sir. As you can doubtless envisage, our departure from the scene of our recent labors was of necessity hurried and—"

"Why don't you go back over the river and light a fire to dry your clothes, Devil-san?" Tommy suggested. "I'll go after the Indian who escaped and try to fetch your horse back."

"That's the first intelligent suggestion I've heard," Corrinne declared. "And it's what we're going to do."

"I warn you that we may as well accede, sir," Hallistead told the Texian. "When my dear lady makes up her mind, nothing we mere men can do or say will shake her."

"Whatever you say then, ma'am," Ole Devil drawled, favoring the woman with a courtly bow. "Go to it, Tommy. And you'd better find out how far away the rest of the Hopis are while you're at it."

"I wonder, sir, if we could have the loan of transportation?" Hallistead inquired, before the little Oriental could turn away. "We've lost our horses and are afoot."

"I'll leave this one for you," Tommy offered, swinging from his borrowed mount.

Having collected the telescope from the pocket of Ole Devil's cloak coat, which was strapped to the cantle of the linebacked dun gelding's saddle, the little Oriental mounted his horse and rode away. After the entertainer had fetched two sets of bulky saddlebags from the bushes in which his wife had hidden, they both climbed on the animal that had been left for them and accompanied Ole Devil to the eastern bank of the river. Knowing that there would no longer be any purpose in trying to conceal their presence, the two men gathered wood and managed to set it on fire. Standing close, so the flames would warm him and, if time was permitted, dry his garments, Ole Devil requested a continuation of the explanation that Hallistead had started to give before Corrinne's intervention.

"Firstly, sir," the entertainer commenced, having seated his wife on the saddlebags after removing the means to reload his pistol, "although I can only give you my word that what I am going to tell you is the truth, I joined Johnson at my own request and with General Houston's wholehearted approval. Of course, the very nature of the task I was performing precluded a truthful explanation of my motives."

"The general needed to find out just exactly what Johnson was up to," Corrinne stated, wanting to ensure that there was no doubt in the young Texian's mind regarding her husband's behavior. "And if it hadn't been for Manny, the invasion by Mexico would have been made weeks ago."

"I did my modest best, sir," the entertainer continued, throwing a look filled with gratitude at the woman who had endured so much for him without complaint or protest. "Without allowing myself to be identified as the culprit, I commenced by starting rumors that a large number of volunteers would soon be forthcoming and their assistance would greatly enhance our chances of success. When these failed to materialize, I hoped to capitalize upon the general disappointment, persuade them to give up the ill-conceived venture, and attach themselves to the rest of the army, even if only to the extent of joining the garrison at Fort Defiance. Regrettably I learned of von Löwenbräu's mission too late to send a message warning the consignment's escort that he was coming. However, on hearing that *you*, sir, were in command, I was sanguine that it would not succeed. If it had, nothing further could have prevented the invasion from being launched. On the other hand, a failure would in all probability have resulted in what I was striving to achieve, the abandonment of the scheme."

"It failed, but not before I'd had to kill von Löwenbräu," Ole Devil said flatly. "And if he'd held off for another five minutes, that needn't have happened."

"I doubt if anybody of consequence and perception will hold his death against you, sir," Hallistead replied, and his wife nodded vigorous agreement. "Knowing him, I'm certain that he left you with no other choice but to do what you did."

"How about the attack?" Ole Devil wanted to know, his every instinct suggesting that the entertainer had been speaking the truth and was sincere. "I was told that Johnson and all his command, or just about, had been wiped out."

"A gross exaggeration, sir," Hallistead corrected. "I'd be surprised if more than fifty of them were killed or have fallen into the enemy's hands.[3] We were, I admit, very nearly taken by surprise. Johnson's men were growing disenchanted by his leadership—or lack of it—and discipline was practically non-existent. So word that a large Mexican force was in the offing arrived much later than would have been the case if the few patrols which had been sent out were performing their duties correctly. When the attack came, all was confusion. There was some resistance, but the majority of those present cut and ran. I—"

"Manny only left as soon as he did because of me and to make sure that you were warned," Corrinne interrupted, once again wanting to set the record straight on her husband's behalf. "Before that what little resistance there was had been organized by him. Johnson had gone and—"

"I don't question Mr. Hallistead's courage, ma'am," Ole Devil assured the woman, smiling warmly. "And I'm satisfied that he acted throughout with the best interests of Texas in mind."

"My thanks, sir," the entertainer boomed, and as he noticed with relief that there was a distinct improvement in the young Texian's attitude toward him, his own tone showed his thanks were more than just a formal response. "We remained unnoticed in the vicinity while I was ascertaining something of the enemy's strength. I regret that my knowledge of matters material is insufficient for me to go into greater detail, but there appeared to be one regiment each of regular artillery, cavalry, and infantry, the cavalry being lancers. In addition, there were one foot and one mounted *activos* or some other form of volunteer regiments. After I had dispatched one of my men to alert Fannin to the danger and sent the other to General Houston with a full report of what had taken place, Corrinne and I made our way toward

3. The actual figure proved to have been sixteen killed and twenty-one—who were subsequently executed by a firing squad—taken prisoner. Colonel Johnson was among those who made good their escape, arriving at Fort Defiance, Goliad, q.v., on February 29, 1836.

Santa Cristóbal Bay. We intended to turn back von Löwenbräu, if he should have succeeded in his purpose, or to warn
you in the more than likely—in our opinions—event that you
had thwarted him."

"*Gracias*, sir," Ole Devil drawled, pleased with the compli-
ment. He turned to let his rear side receive the benefit of the
fire and glanced at the woman. "Please excuse my back,
ma'am."

"Think nothing of it, Captain, I only hope that you'll have
time to get properly dried," Corrinne answered, showing
more grace now that she was satisfied the Texian was regarding her husband favorably. "Tell him the rest, Manny, dar-
ling."

"With the greatest of pleasure, my dove." Hallistead assented. "We arrived just in time to see von Löwenbräu's
party taking their departure. From his and your absence, we
concluded, correctly as has been proved, that you had circumvented his schemes and dispensed with their dubious
services. So we sought out the tracks left by your party, not a
difficult task in itself, and followed. Unfortunately first Corrinne's and then my mount foundered, and we were left
afoot, but we kept on undaunted."

"You had bad luck," Ole Devil commiserated, with a sym-
pathetic glance at the exhausted-looking woman, but he was
also seeing how the loss of their horses added to his difficulties.

"It had its compensations," Corrinne replied.

"Very true, light of my life," Hallistead agreed. "And
there was one consolation, sir. My dear lady wife was attired
for walking, a precaution we both had considered advisable
before taking our leave of San Patricio. What was more, as
we appreciated the necessity of traveling light, we brought
away little apart from our invaluable makeup equipment and
a change of raiment for her. All our possessions are in the
saddlebags."

"I'm sorry to hear you lost everything else, ma'am," Ole
Devil remarked, knowing that the couple's fame had been

founded on their excellent disguise, quick-change, and impersonation act, involving numerous wigs and sets of appropriate clothing.

"It's not as bad as that." Corrinne smiled, being far from displeased by the Texian's obvious concern. "We left the majority of our costumes in General Houston's care and brought away all that mattered."

"Knowing the precarious nature of what we were intending to do, I considered the course to be judicious," Hallistead elaborated. "Then, if we needed to flee, all would not be lost."

Amused by the entertainer's pedantic and bombastic way of speaking, Ole Devil allowed him to carry on with the explanation in his own fashion. On reaching the stream, the couple had heard horses beyond it. Telling his wife to hide with their property and leaving her the blunderbuss for protection, Hallistead had climbed into the silver maple, meaning to discover who was coming. Before he could satisfy his curiosity, he had seen the Hopis approaching on foot and realized that they were stalking the men whose appearance he was awaiting. The Texian knew the rest of the story.

While listening, Ole Devil was considering the latest developments. The fact that the Arizona Hopi Activos Regiment was almost certainly much closer than he had anticipated meant he must return to the mule train as quickly as possible.

Doing so with only three horses between four people was going to be difficult.

10

THE TEXIAN WITH THE FACE
OF *EL DIABLO*

Although a person who had been acquainted with Tommy Okasi only in his capacity of valet might have questioned the wisdom of the decision, Ole Devil Hardin had not had the slightest qualms over sending him in search of the Arizona Hopi Activos Regiment. In fact, the Texian was confident that he was more than equal to the task.

Before he had been compelled to leave his homeland with no possibility of ever returning,[1] the little Oriental had been a fully qualified samurai.[2] The power and authority of the

1. While attending the twenty-first Annual Convention of Western Writers of America at Fort Worth, Texas, in 1974 and during a second visit the following year, the author tried to discover what had caused Tommy Okasi—this was not his real name, but an Americanized corruption of the one he gave when picked up by Captain Jeremiah Hardin's ship—to leave his native land. The members of the Hardin, Fog, and Blaze clan to whom I spoke were adamant that because of the circumstances and the high social standing of the families involved—all of whom have descendants holding positions of influence and importance in Japan at the time of writing—it would be inadvisable even at this late date to make the facts public.

2. Samurai: a member of the lower nobility's elite warrior class, usually acting as a retainer of the daimyos, the hereditary Japanese feudal barons.

formerly highly influential warrior class were already on the wane,[3] but its members still received a very thorough education in many aspects of the martial arts. Not only was he well able to take care of himself in any kind of fight—whether it should be with his nation's traditional weapons, bare-handed employing ju-jitsu and karate, or to a lesser extent, firearms[4] —he was equally competent at performing the exacting duties of a scout.

Holding his big blue-roan[5] gelding at the fastest pace that was compatible with following the tracks of the fleeing Hopi brave and carrying the longbow by hand through the woodland, Tommy kept constantly on the alert. He did not know if his quarry had companions in the vicinity, other than those who had been killed at the small river. So he listened carefully as well as scrutinized the surrounding trees and bushes for signs of possible danger. Before he had covered much more than a hundred yards, he heard the sounds of several horses moving away, but he was far too experienced a warrior to be lulled into a sense of complacency.

From the signs he observed, Tommy deduced that one of the braves had been in advance of the other three as they were coming through the woodland. He had either seen or heard something to make him suspicious, for he had returned to fetch his companions on foot. Further evidence of

3. During the mid-nineteenth century an increasing contact with the Western world was bringing an ever-growing realization that the retention of a hereditary and privileged warrior class was incompatible with the formation of a modern and industrialized society. Various edicts issued by the emperor between 1873 and 1876 abolished the special rights of the samurai, and although some of their traditions and concepts were retained, they ceased to exist as such.
4. Although primitive kinds of firearms had been known in Japan since the arrival of Portuguese explorers in 1543, the samurai had small regard for them, and little time was devoted to learning how to use them.
5. Blue-roan: a horse with a more or less uniform mixture of white and black, or deep mahogany bay-colored hairs over the entire body. If the darker hairs are sorrel—yellowish to red-golden—it is a strawberry roan; if an ordinary bay, a red-roan.

this was given when the little Oriental came to a spot where four horses had been tethered to a clump of bushes. There were torn-off leaves, broken twigs, and other signs to suggest that the fleeing man had paused to snatch free the securing ropes. He was still riding the dead Mexican officer's mount, which he had acquired from Ole Devil, and was apparently leading one of the remainder. Impelled by herd instinct, training, or an open plains-dwelling creature's distaste for wooded country, the other three horses were following.

In spite of the fact that everything he saw suggested that the quartet had constituted the entire scouting party, Tommy pressed onward without any relaxation of his vigilance. He hoped that he would be able to catch up with his quarry and recover at least his employer's reserve horse before going too far. If he could do so, he would deliver it—or them, should he be fortunate enough to obtain more than the one —to Ole Devil for use by the Hallisteads, who were in urgent need of transportation. With that done, he could resume his search for the enemy.

Much to Tommy's unspoken annoyance, the hope did not materialize.

On reaching the fringe of the woodland, the little Oriental saw the Hopi a good three hundred yards ahead. He was traveling in the manner suggested by the tracks. What was more, he clearly had not overlooked the possibility of pursuit. Even as Tommy was emerging from the last of the trees, he gazed over his shoulder. Snapping his head to the front, he immediately encouraged the horse he was sitting and the one he was leading to increase their pace. To add to Tommy's sense of vexation, the three animals, which were running free, stimulated by a yell from the brave, continued to keep pace with their companions.

An expert *kyudoka*, archer, Tommy appreciated the limitations as well as the qualifications of his weapon and skill. Even if an arrow would carry that far and he was fortunate enough to make a hit, it would not retain sufficient impetus to kill or disable the brave or the horse he was sitting. So the only alternative would be to try to ride into a lethal range. Once that had been attained, there would be no need for him to dismount before drawing and loosing a shaft. In spite of the bow's length, it could be used effectively at *yabusame*.[6]

Instead of setting off immediately to make the attempt, Tommy gave rapid thought to the other aspects involved. It was, he realized, impossible for him to reach a shooting distance without a long chase. Nor was there any certainty that he would be able to do so. The Hopi had the advantage of riding a two-mount relay. If—as everything so far had indicated—he was an accomplished horseman, he could transfer from the newly acquired animal to the other while on the move and with little reduction of speed. Against that Tommy would have to push his solitary animal without respite. At the end of the chase, and it was quite possible that he might fail to catch up or be led to the rest of the *activos*, he was faced with the necessity of returning as quickly as possible to pass on the information to his employer.

Reluctantly, for he still retained the samurai's distaste for admitting any task was beyond his capabilities, Tommy conceded that he would be unable to obtain the horses unless something unforeseen should occur. Being a realist, he was unwilling to rely upon such an uncertain eventuality to serve his purpose. So he concluded that the only course left open to him was to carry out the secondary mission of locating the rest of their enemies.

Waiting until the rapidly departing Hopi looked behind again, Tommy shook his bow-filled fist in the air and, with a gesture of disgust, turned his horse and retreated into the woodland. Halting when he was satisfied that he would be

6. *Yabusame:* translated literally, "shooting from a running horse." In competition, the mounted *kyudoka* rides at a gallop over a course 2 *cho*—roughly 238 yards—in length, along which are placed at approximately 38, 118, and 193 yards, 2-foot-square wooden targets on posts between 36 and 48 inches high. Traditionally, the *kyudoka* discharges—from a distance of around 30 feet—an arrow with a forked head that shatters under the impact of a hit.

concealed by the trees, he saw nothing to suggest his true purpose had been suspected. Showing no sign of slowing down, much less coming back, the brave was disappearing over a distant fold of the ground.

Setting his roan into motion, the little Oriental once more took up the pursuit. However, he traveled in a vastly different manner. Now his purpose was to follow undetected rather than to catch up and attack. For all that, while he had not done so earlier, now he nocked an arrow to the bow's string. If he had need of the weapon, it would be quickly, and there might not be time for him to remove and set it up when trouble came.

Advancing cautiously, Tommy studied the terrain ahead with great care. As he followed in the general direction taken by the Hopi, he took advantage of every available scrap of cover. When he had to cross a skyline, he first ensured that he could do so without running the risk of being seen by his would-be quarry. At intervals he caught glimpses of the brave. However, from the other's behavior, he was confident that he had not been seen in return.

After having covered about six miles in such a fashion, Tommy was treated to a suggestion that he was approaching the rest of the *activos*. Halting behind a clump of bushes, he watched the scout talking with half a dozen more Hopi braves and pointing toward him. For a moment he wondered if he had been less successful in avoiding being noticed than he believed. One of the warriors seemed to be urging the rest to advance. However, another—the oldest, if his gray hair was any guide—declined. Turning their horses, they accompanied the scout toward where more riders were appearing on the horizon.

Employing even greater stealth and care, the little Oriental followed the latest party of Hopis. Noticing a small knoll that seemed well suited to his needs, he headed toward it. Leaving his roan concealed and ground hitched behind the knoll, he returned the arrow to his quiver. Taking the telescope from his saddlebags, he carried it and the bow with him as he made the ascent. On reaching the top, he found he had an ideal point of vantage. Flattening on his stomach behind a rock, he laid the bow at his side and opened the telescope.

Half a mile from Tommy's hiding place, halted on the banks of a stream, was a mass of men and horses. Using the telescope, he gave them a closer examination than was possible with the naked eye. One glance was sufficient to stifle any slight hopes he might have cherished. He had found the main body of the Arizona Hopi Activos Regiment.

What was more, there was a much greater number than Ole Devil had anticipated!

At least three hundred braves and twenty or more Mexicans, Tommy estimated as he scanned them through the powerful magnification of the telescope. His employer had assumed there would be two hundred at the most.

From what the little Oriental could make out, on the basis of his experiences with the Texas Light Cavalry, the return of the scout and advance party had caused a halt to be called. While the majority of the Hopis were attending to the horses, some of their chiefs—who acted as noncoms and could be identified by the necklaces and bracelets of silver inlaid with turquoise blue gemstones they sported—and all the Mexicans were gathered around the survivor. Among them, he could recognize the man who had captured and been on the point of torturing his employer when he had intervened and effected a rescue. The man had escaped then and again after the battle at Santa Cristóbal Bay. From what Tommy could make out, it was he who was doing most of the talking.

*　*　*

"It was the Texian with the face of *el diablo*, señores!" the surviving scout announced dramatically, making the sign of the cross as he had been taught to do when mentioning the devil by the mission fathers.

Although the words were addressed to the whole group assembled around him, the brave was looking straight into the face of the Arizona Hopi Activos Regiment's current commanding officer. He had just completed a description of the events at the small river which confirmed the conclusions that Tommy Okasi had formed from reading their tracks.

A low and furious snarl burst from Major—recently promoted by virtue of his skill with a sword and willingness to demonstrate it to the unofficial rank of colonel—Abrahán Felipe Gonzales de Villena y Danvila's prominent Hapsburg lips, which stemmed from the result of an indiscretion on the part of a female ancestor. Unconsciously his right hand rose to touch the severed end of one of the long, flowing plumes of emerald green tail feathers from a cock quetzal[7] attached to the top of his black astrakhan hussar-style busby.

All too well Villena remembered how the damage had been inflicted by a bullet from the remarkable rifle belonging to the "Texian with the face of *el diablo*," although it had been in the hands of the strange little foreigner who had proved to be such a terribly efficient and deadly warrior. He should have been grateful for having had a narrow escape, but he was not. In addition to having to flee from them, he had left behind his magnificent Toledo steel *épée-de-combat*, which he carried instead of the more cumbersome cavalry saber. While he had subsequently retrieved the weapon, which they had not carried off for some reason,[8] he would never forgive either of them for inflicting such a humiliation. Nor would he cease to hate them as long as they lived.

Slightly over medium height, with a physique that was reasonable without being exceptional, Villena was in his late twenties. Scion of an extremely wealthy family, he was trucu-

7. Quetzal: *Pharomachrus mocino*, one of the Trogoniformes order of birds, found in the mountain forests of Central and South America and regarded as sacred by various Indian nations in those regions. Two of the cock's fringed tail covert features may attain a length of over three feet each, making them much sought after for decorative purposes.
8. Being in a hurry to rejoin the mule train, Ole Devil Hardin and Tommy Okasi had not taken the *épée-de-combat* because neither had wished to be encumbered by carrying it without a sheath.

lent, proud, and overbearing. His deeply bronzed and handsome face was marred by cold hazel eyes with somewhat
drooping lids and an arrogant expression. Apart from being
light green instead of yellow and having a few other minor
differences, his uniform—which had been accepted as the
official attire for the officers because his father had financed
the formation of the regiment[9]—was modeled upon the late-
eighteenth-century Spanish Army's Olivenza Hussars, in
which, during the Napoleonic Wars, one of his forebears had
been a colonel.[10]

"Well, *gentlemen*," Villena purred, in the icily polite yet
mockingly impolite way he always adopted toward those he
regarded as his inferiors, "it appears that *I* was correct about
the actions of the rebel scum."

On rejoining the surviving seven companies after the defeat of the three which had made the disastrous attack at
Santa Cristóbal Bay, Villena had announced that he was taking command and intended to avenge their dead comrades-
in-arms. Using a chance comment that might have been construed as implying he had shown cowardice as an excuse, he
had killed the only officer senior to him in a duel. That had
served as a warning to any other potential dissidents. Knowing his quick and savage temper, as well as his deadly skill
with a sword or a pistol, they had taken the hint, and there
had been no further objections to his proposals.

However, some slight demur had been expressed when
Villena called for comments upon the proposals he had out-
lined for achieving vengeance. The general consensus had
been divided on the matter of where the Texians might be
located. Although it had been accepted they could no longer

9. Possibly so that, in the event of anything going wrong, there would be a
scapegoat other than his son, Villena's father had appointed an older man
with military training—who had subsequently fallen during the battle at
Santa Cristóbal Bay—to be the commanding officer of the Arizona Hopi
Activos Regiment.
10. Colonel José Gonzáles de Villena y Danvila. See Chapter XIII of *A
Ship of the Line* by C. S. Forester.

be found at the bay, that was the only point upon which there had been unanimous agreement. Some of the officers had believed they would take a route to the northwest and deliver the consignment of rifles to the retreating main body of the Republic of Texas's army. Others had considered that they would travel in a southwesterly direction with the garrison at Fort Defiance as their destination.

Showing a surprising forethought, Villena had disagreed with both schools of thought. He had the advantage of knowing the nature of the man who had briefly been his prisoner and who appeared to be in command of the consignment. So he had decided that neither was likely to be the true objective. Or even if Goliad had been the satanic-faced Texian's original goal, knowing that the *activos* were likely to be between him and it, he would not take the most direct route. On the other hand, it was improbable that Major General Samuel Houston would want the rifles taken to him while he was withdrawing. Rather, he would have arranged for them to be transported to a prearranged rendezvous. The most likely point, in Villena's opinion, would be the "capital" city of the so-called republic: Washington-on-the-Brazos. With that in mind, he had led his regiment in the appropriate direction.

"But if—as that is the case, M— Colonel," the major commanding Company Five put in, making the corrections to his phrasing of the question and the honorific when he remembered how touchy the other was on such points, "why was the Texian coming in this direction?"

"He has left his command to carry out a scouting mission once before," Villena explained, having no idea that a second and larger force of the Mexican Army was operating not too far away.[11] Swinging a threatening gaze at them which

11. The second Mexican column was the Tamaulipa Brigade under the command of General José Urrea, who was to gain notoriety for his inhuman treatment of prisoners. In addition to having the twenty-one surrenderers executed at San Patricio, he later ordered the cold-blooded

dared the rest of the officers to comment upon how he had gained his information regarding the Texian, he turned his attention to the scout. "Did either of them follow you?"

"No, señor," the brave replied, and, having failed to see Tommy Okasi on the occasions when he had looked behind him, believed he was speaking the truth.

"They'll be going back to the mule train as quickly as they can now they know we're so close," Company Five's commanding officer suggested.

"Then we'll go after them as soon as the horses are rested, *if* that meets with your approval, *Major* Santoval," Villena answered, his tone and attitude filled with menace and offense. Once again, there was no response to his challenge, and he looked at the group of Hopi war leaders. "Chief Tomás, send twelve of your best men ahead to find the rebels. Tell the rest that we will soon catch those who killed their brothers and they will soon be able to extract a terrible revenge."

---

slaughter of almost four hundred Texians who had fallen into his hands at Goliad.

11
YOU'LL HAVE TO LEAVE NOW

"Well, there's Hickert's Landing and the ferry," Ole Devil Hardin remarked, pointing down the long and gentle slope that he and his companions were about to descend. He paused and turned to gaze back for several seconds in the direction from which they had come. To anybody who knew him well, there was a noticeable anxiety in the apparently unemotional words with which he went on. "But no sign of Tommy yet."

"Would the continued absence of your worthy Oriental factotum be advantageous or otherwise, Devil?" Mangrove Hallistead inquired, having dropped the formal "sir" during the long and arduous hours of traveling in the young Texian's company, but, even tired though he was, retaining his usual verbosity, as he and his wife trudged alongside the lathered and leg-weary horse that had been left for them by Tommy Okasi.

"It could be good," Ole Devil admitted. "The longer he's away, the farther he's had to go to find the Hopis and the more time we'll have before they can reach us."

"In that eventuality, finding themselves faced with a

lengthy and extended pursuit, might they not turn back?"
Hallistead suggested, without mentioning the possibility that
Tommy might be unable to return.

"They might," Ole Devil conceded, grasping his linebacked dun gelding's saddle horn and reaching for the stirrup iron with his left foot. "But I don't mean to count on it.
Let's get down to the landing stage and over the river."

"Does that mean I get to ride again?" Corrinne Hallistead
asked.

"Unless you'd rather run alongside," Ole Devil replied
with a grin, swinging astride the dun.

"I'm not sure which would be most preferable right now."
The little woman sighed, waiting for her husband to mount
the borrowed horse so she could get on behind him. "But
knowing you pair, I'll probably be expected to dance for your
entertainment when we get to the other side. Do you know
something, Devil? My mother actually warned me against
marrying into the 'thittuh.' "

"Up you come, light of my life," Hallistead boomed, helping his wife board the animal. "Didn't I promise you would
travel extensively and see strange and exotic places of interest?"

"Yes, dear," Corrinne agreed, wrapping her arms around
the entertainer's waist. "But you didn't say I'd have to do it
this way. I don't know which is most sore, my feet or my—
well, somewhere else."

Glancing at the little woman, Ole Devil felt nothing but
the greatest admiration for her. Once his clothes had dried,
he had decided against waiting for Tommy to rejoin them.
So he had fastened the Hallisteads' belongings to the cantle
of the dun's saddle, reducing some of the weight to be carried by the horse which they both would have to ride. They
had set the best pace possible, while also conserving sufficient energy to leave the couple's heavily ladened mount
particularly with something in hand to be used if there
should be a need for greater speed. It had entailed their
walking and leading the animals for long periods. Despite

clearly being very tired, Corrinne had refused to continue riding on such occasions. Instead, not only had she trudged mile after weary mile at her husband's side, but she had also managed to keep her spirits up and had never complained.

Apart from the effort that it required, the journey from the woodland had gone by uneventfully. Throughout it, especially in the later stages, Ole Devil had expected Tommy to catch up with them. However, with about two more hours of daylight left, they had come into sight of Hickert's Landing, and he still had not put in an appearance. In spite of being aware of the little Oriental's ability as a fighting man and appreciating the possible benefits from it, the Texian had grown increasingly perturbed by his continued absence.

Wanting to take his thoughts from Tommy, Ole Devil studied their destination about three-quarters of a mile ahead. Because of the flow of traffic attracted by the ferry, a small community had grown up around its owner's premises on the eastern bank of the San Bernard River. However, as Ole Devil knew from his earlier visit, with one exception all of the population other than the Hickert family had already taken their departure.

From what the young Texian could see, Moses Hickert had taken to heart his warning that the second Mexican column —or at least a force from it—might already be moving north from San Patricio and, even if they were not, the Arizona Hopi Activos Regiment was almost certain to come in search of the mule train. A couple of wagons, which had been under the lean-to when he and Tommy had left that morning, were now standing in front of the house. He regarded the sight as a good sign. The owner of the ferry had stated an intention of continuing to operate it for as long as possible in case it should be needed to carry refugees fleeing to safety from the Mexicans. However, as he had obviously taken the precaution of making ready to leave, he was likely to be willing to accept that the time for departure had come.

There was, however, something just as important as the preparations for departure from Ole Devil's point of view.

Several saddle mounts, he hoped more than the family would consider necessary for their requirements, were mingling with the draft horses in the large corral. Provided that Hickert could be persuaded to part with some of the surplus, one of his problems would be eased.

As he and his companions were drawing nearer, Ole Devil turned his attention to the means by which they would go across the 250-yard-wide deep river. Not only must he convince the Hickerts that the time had come for them to leave, but he must induce them to destroy their source of income. All too well he knew that he must employ persuasion. He would be dealing with a man who possessed a full measure of the typical Texian's spirit of rugged individualism and disinclination to take orders. So any attempt to dictate orders to Hickert would end in failure.

The ferry was a flat-bottomed boat, completely decked over with stout planks and having sturdy guardrails along each side. Provided that their teams were unhitched, it could accommodate two fully loaded twenty-six-foot-long Conestoga pattern[1] freight wagons. However, as the river's current along that section was exceedingly sluggish, it could not be operated on the more economical compass system.[2] Instead, a powerful cable of rope passed under the deck—being secured at the bow and stern—and very tightly around a massive pulley wheel on each bank. The wheel at the eastern side was equipped with a long, thick crossbar and had a ramp

1. Conestoga wagon: one that is large, very heavily built, with its bed higher at each end than in the middle so that its contents would not spill out when going up and down hills. Its dull white canvas cover had a similar curve, but to a more pronounced degree. The wheels were broad, as an aid to going across country where there were no trails. Also called a scoop wagon.
2. Compass system ferry: Instead of being hauled across the river in a straight line, the boat was held at the required angle by guy ropes at each end and utilized the pressure of the current against the sides to swing it in an arc from one bank to the other. It could be used only on comparatively narrow rivers but was cheaper as it did not need any other form of motive power.

over the two portions of the cable, so that a pair of draft oxen could be hitched on and supply the motive power.

Noticing that the boat was alongside the opposite landing stage and wanting to avoid any delay in going over, Ole Devil drew the Manton pistol from its loop on his belt and fired a shot into the air. The two male figures working in the corral stared. Then one of them pointed across the river and shouted something that did not reach the approaching riders' ears. Clearly he had announced their coming. Two more men stepped from the porch of the house, and a woman appeared at the end of one of the wagons.

Even at that distance Ole Devil could identify the people on the other bank. The two men who were already leaving the corral were, as might be expected, big and bulky. Their parents, Maw and Moses Hickert, stood respectively six feet and six feet two in height and weighed over four hundred pounds between them. While he was pleased to see the members of the family, he was less enamored of the fifth person who was present.

Nothing Ole Devil had seen of Abel Ferris the previous evening had been calculated to produce a feeling of liking. Somewhat smaller than any of the Hickerts, which did not make him anywhere close to being classed as a midget, he had struck the Texian as being a bullying hardcase and potential troublemaker. Unlike the male members of the Hickert family, who wore town-bought shirts, trousers, and heavy boots, he had on smoke-blackened and greasy buckskins. A cheap bowie knife, even larger than the far superior James Black's product carried by Ole Devil, hung in a fancy Indian sheath on his belt.

Giving a wave, Hickert returned to the porch and collected two oxgoads. He handed one to his wife, and they went to where two big draft oxen were standing patiently in harness. At his command, without needing inducement from the steel-tipped poles, the animals began to plod ponderously in a circle around the wheel. As it turned and the cable began to pay out, the boat moved forward. Before Ole Devil

and his party had arrived, it was waiting for them at the
western landing stage. Already the Hickerts were making
preparations for the return trip. He observed that although
Ferris had accompanied the couple, they alone set about the
task of uncoupling and turning the oxen around. Nor did the
surly hardcase offer to help as they set about refastening the
beasts' harnesses to the wheel's crossbar. Instead, he stood
scowling across the river. Once the passengers had led their
mounts aboard, the oxen were started walking in the opposite direction, and the boat reversed its course toward the
eastern bank.

"Howdy, Cap'n Hardin," Hickert greeted, as the Texian
walked from the landing stage with the dun following on his
heels like a well-trained hound dog. "You're back a whole
heap sooner'n you counted on."

"With cause, sir," Ole Devil replied, conscious of the way
that the owner of the ferry was looking at the Hallisteads but
wanting to establish the urgency of his return before satisfying his curiosity. "We found the Hopis are much closer than
I'd been led to assume. In fact, they're likely to be here
before noon tomorrow."

"As soon's that?" Hickert asked, rubbing a huge hand
across his bristle-stubbled chin and looking at his boat.

"I don't think it will be much longer," Ole Devil replied,
doubting whether the scouts with whom he had come into
contact would be more than ten miles ahead of the main
body. Then he turned his gaze to the big, buxom, and, in
spite of being in her early fifties, still-handsome wife of the
ferry's owner, continuing, "Mr. and Mrs. Hallistead here
have been trav—"

"Missus—" Maw Hickert repeated, staring at the small
figure alongside the entertainer with first surprise, then en-
lightenment and pity. "Landsakes! So you are. Come on up
to the house, gal. You look 'most dead on your feet."

"I feel it," Corrinne admitted with a wry smile, sensing
and appreciating the larger woman's feeling of compassion
for her condition, as she walked forward slowly. "But I'd

rather just *feel* it than be it, which could have happened if we'd stayed at San Patricio."

"San Patri—" Maw began, eyes raking Corrinne from head to toe, and being sufficiently experienced to read the signs correctly, she could tell the whole story without needing to take the hard-used condition of the horses into consideration. Raising her voice in a bellow which, Ole Devil decided, would not have shamed Stentor,[3] she called, "Henry! Clyde! Get on down here pronto and take care of these good folks's hosses." Then, moderating her tone, she went on. "You come along with me and rest whatever you figure needs resting, gal. We can leave the talking to the menfolks. Only, don't you go wasting too much time on it, Mose. These folks've been traveling fast 'n' hard, so they could likely do with a rest."

"Go ahead, my dove," Hallistead prompted when his wife looked at him for guidance. "I'll follow you eftsoons with these gentlemen."

"So you reckon's it's as bad as all that, huh, Cap'n?" Hickert asked as the women were walking away.

"I do, sir," Ole Devil confirmed. "You'll have to move out now."

"Have to?" Ferris repeated before Hickert could speak. He advanced to stand by the owner of the ferry's side and eyed the young Texian truculently. "Well, now, soldier boy, I can't say's how Mose 'n' me've ever took kindly to letting *nobody* tell *us*'s we *have* to do anything."

Listening to the harsh Louisiana drawl, Ole Devil decided that Ferris must have understood his meaning. When making the statement, he had had no intention of giving orders to Hickert. He was merely making a comment based upon the conversation they had had the previous night.

"Just how soon do you conclude they'll be getting here,

3. Stentor: according to Grecian mythology and Homer's *Iliad,* a Greek herald in the Trojan War whose voice had the volume of fifty men.

Cap'n?" Hickert inquired before the Texian could attempt to
clear up Ferris's misapprehension.

"It could be tonight or sometime tomorrow, sir." Ole
Devil guessed, wishing he could give a more positive reply.
"I won't know for sure until—"

"Have you seen 'em?" Ferris demanded, with an air of
challenge.

"We had a run-in with their scouts, killed three and one
got away," Ole Devil answered, speaking in a polite way
which would have warned anybody who had had much contact with him that he was growing annoyed by the interrup-
tions. "I sent my man after him, with orders to find the rest
of them."

"Your man!" Ferris snorted, his whole attitude redolent of
contempt. "You hear that, Mose. The soldier boy's sent that
heathen Chinese and's counting on him to find out how close
them Injuns be."

"Tommy's as good a scout as any man I know," Ole Devil
declared, but he appreciated that unless seen in action, the
little Oriental was not an impressive figure. He was also
aware that the kind of Chinese with whom either of the men
had come into contact with before were not noted for ability
in the martial arts. "I'm satisfied that he'll find them if anybody can."

"*You* might be, soldier boy," Ferris sneered, his voice ooz-
ing offense and disdain, "but that don't mean's how anybody
else has to."

Listening to the challenge in the derisive words, Ole Devil
realized that the burly hardcase was bent on causing trouble
and wondered why this should be. To the best of his knowledge, they had never met before the previous evening, and
the name Ferris meant nothing to him. Although he had
been conscious of the other eying him malevolently yesterday evening, he had thought little of it. During his life he had
come across men who harbored a deep and bitter resentment against anybody in a position of authority or who was
better favored in wealth, social standing, and possessions

than themselves. So he had been inclined to regard Ferris as such a person and had ignored him. Now he was wondering if the hardcase had some other reason for trying to pick a fight. He also appreciated that under the circumstances, it was up to him to avoid becoming involved in one if possible.

While there were those who believed differently, Ole Devil was neither quick-tempered nor the kind of hothead who went out of his way to seek trouble. He had been born and raised in the state of Louisiana, which was notorious as being a hotbed for adherents of the code duello, but he had been taught that fighting and killing were matters to be taken seriously. They should never be indulged in on the flimsy pretenses used by many wealthy young southrons as excuses to issue challenges to duels. So he refused to allow his resentment over the doubts which Ferris was casting upon his veracity, or Tommy's abilities, to make him lose his temper.

For all his resolve, Ole Devil realized that avoiding a contretemps with the hardcase would not be easy. A shrewd judge of character, he had formed an accurate assessment of the other's nature. What was more, experience had taught him that there was only one way to deal with such a man. Any suggestion of hesitation or attempts at temporizing were likely to be regarded as a sign of weakness and would probably lead to further abuses.

There was, however, an additional factor for the young Texian to take into consideration. If he tried to evade the issue, apart from the likelihood of causing additional aggression on Ferris's part, he might forfeit Hickert's respect. In that case, his advice and wishes would be ignored. Or at least there could be such a delay in acting upon them that it might result in the ferry's falling into the enemy's hands. That would endanger the lives of everybody present, as well as lessen the time needed by the Hopis to catch up with the mule train. He was counting upon the destruction of the boat to allow him to rejoin the consignment and prepare for the fight which he believed was sure to come. Nor could he order that the wrecking of the family's business be carried out. The only way he could achieve his purpose was by gaining their support.

A glance at Moses Hickert warned Ole Devil that his assumption was correct. While he sensed a disapproval of Ferris's behavior behind the seamed, tanned, and expressionless face, he knew there would be no help out of his predicament from that source. According to the code by which the ferryboat's owner lived, any personal matter must be settled between the two main participants and without outside interference.

Even as Ole Devil accepted that he must take some kind of action, he was all too aware of what doing so would entail. He would be contending with a man who matched him in height but was heavier. Furthermore, while he was tired from the exertions of the past day, Ferris was fresh and rested.

In spite of all that, the young Texian knew he must do something.

And soon!

12

ISN'T THIS JUST LIKE *MEN*?

"Couldn't be sure this far off, Cap'n," Moses Hickert re-marked, almost casually, as the grim-faced young Texian was about to release the linebacked dun gelding's reins as a pre-lude to tackling his tormentor. "But it sure looks like the lil Chinee feller of your'n coming."

"It *is* Tommy," Mangrove Hallistead confirmed, having been standing silently but experiencing a growing concern over what was developing. He had heard of his companion's reputation of being a "lil ole devil for a fight" and doubted whether the other would have sufficient self-control to avoid one in spite of being on an important mission. However, he had not been able to think of a way in which he could inter-vene and prevent it. "He'll soon be here, the way he's rid-ing."

"*Bueno*," Ole Devil Hardin replied, without taking his eyes from Abel Ferris's surly face, but directing the words at the other men. "Once he arrives and we hear what he has to say, we'll know what has to be done."

"Yeah?" the hardcase growled, eager to cause a fight but also wanting to have what would pass as a reason for doing so. Remembering the stories he had heard about his proposed victim, he did not doubt that he could achieve this. "Only we'll make up our own minds. This here ain't Iberville Parish,[1] Louisiana, where everybody has to jump when one of you Hardin, Fog, and Blaze bunch beckons."

At the mention of the region in the United States where his clan had their most extensive holdings, Ole Devil realized that he might be wrong regarding the cause of Ferris's hostility. Up until then he had put it down to stemming from either just a bad-tempered desire to make trouble or—as when a man deliberately sought out and challenged a successful duelist—a matter of wanting to prove himself better than somebody who had earned a reputation for being a tough and capable fighter.

Other possibilities now sprang to Ole Devil's mind. Ferris's Louisiana accent suggested what might be a solution. He could be nursing a grudge against the members of the Hardin, Fog, and Blaze clan for some real or fancied wrong and was hoping for an opportunity to repay it.

It was also feasible, the young Texian decided, that the hardcase might have an even more sinister intent. After Ole Devil had left Louisiana, a reward had been offered for his arrest and return.[2] However, it had been for a comparatively small amount and would be paid only if he were taken back alive. So, particularly with Texas in such a state of turmoil, Ferris was unlikely to be considering making such an attempt. He could have something else in mind, believing that if he could kill Ole Devil, the people who had put up the reward—and whose son he had been falsely accused of murdering—might be generous out of gratitude for having such a service rendered when they had no other means of taking revenge.

No matter what Ferris's actual motives might be, Ole Devil knew that nothing was changing in the situation he was

1. The state of Louisiana uses the word *parish* instead of *county*.
2. See footnote 5 on page 4.

trying to bring about. Except that if the latter eventuality should be correct, he would be meaning to kill rather than merely assert his superiority by physical means.

The possibility that the hardcase was hoping to earn the Beaucoup family's appreciation and financial support made dealing with him more difficult. Although Ole Devil had not envisaged that he might need one, on the way to the ferry he had instinctively exchanged the pistol used to signal their coming for the loaded weapon in his saddle holster. So he had the means to defend himself and in a fashion that would in all probability come as a complete surprise to his antagonist.

Unfortunately the issue was not as simple as that.

Ole Devil realized that he could be making the wrong assumption. Perhaps Ferris was only a bully trying to assert himself or, at the worst, wanting to work off some ill feeling toward the Hardin, Fog, and Blaze clan in general by picking a fistfight with one of its members who had crossed his path. In that case he would be contemplating not a murderous assault but merely a roughhouse brawl.

While Ole Devil was willing to be completely ruthless where the protection of the consignment was concerned, he had never regarded lightly the taking of another human being's life for personal reasons. So he could not adopt the most obvious course of drawing his pistol and ending the matter with a bullet.

"I'd be obliged if you'd have the ferry across there when my man arrives, Mr. Hickert," Ole Devil requested, giving no sign of his thoughts or even that he had heard Ferris's comment.

"Sure, Cap'n," Hickert assented, without showing the slightest indication of how he felt about what was happening. "I'll tend to it."

"Now me," Ferris said, advancing a pace, "I'm wondering why, with you being so concerned about them Hopis 'n' all, you didn't go look for 'em yourself instead of sending that heathen Chinee."

"We can only hope that they're not too close," Ole Devil drawled, dropping the dun's reins and starting to turn toward the river, still apparently refusing to acknowledge his challenger's presence. "The farther they're away—"

"God damn it!" the burly hardcase bellowed, continuing to advance and his face darkening with anger at being subjected to such cavalier treatment. "I'm talking to you, you fancy-dressed son—"

Instantly, satisfied that the other was behaving as he had anticipated and had sought to bring about, Ole Devil pivoted around with such violence that his hat was dislodged to fall back on his shoulders, and he sprang to meet Ferris.

Taken completely unawares, the hardcase was further disconcerted by the exposure of the hornlike tufts of hair on the sides of the young Texian's head. They added to the already savage Mephistophelian aspect of his face that was enhanced by the strain of the exertions he had endured during his present assignment. For the first time Ferris began to realize what was portended by the second part of Ole Devil's sobriquet. Although far from religious, he was sufficiently superstitious for the shock to numb his responses at a moment when they should have been working at their fastest.

Up lashed Ole Devil's right arm, delivering a backhand blow with wicked force to the side of the burly man's left cheek. Alarm as much as pain caused Ferris to snatch his forward leg to the rear so as to carry himself away from his satanic-featured assailant. Almost before the foot had touched the ground, the flat palm whipped across to meet his head as it was turned by the force of the blow and reversed its direction with an equal violence. Once again, the recipient of the attack was driven to make an involuntary withdrawal and with even more disastrous results. Lashing around, driven by the full power and fury of a wiry and whipcord-strong body, the knuckles repeated their contact with no loss of velocity for all the speed that they were moving.

Coming so rapidly and hard, the blows completely destroyed Ferris's equilibrium. Trying to back away with suffi-

cient haste to avoid further punishment and not a little
frightened by the almost demoniac rage which he had caused
to be released, he lost his footing. Going down, he alighted
on his rump with a bone-jarring thud. For a few seconds he
sat dazed and winded. Then, although his vision was still
blurred, he spit out an obscenity, and his right hand went
toward the hilt of his knife.

"Go ahead!" a savage voice challenged, cutting like the
blast of an icy cold wind into the mists of anger, pain, and
humiliation that were tearing through the discomforted
hardcase. "Take it out—if you think you can."

Before the final part of the speech was completed, Ferris's
vision cleared, and the sight that met his eyes was one he
would never forget. Crouching slightly, the tall figure before
him was charged with a grim and terrible menace. What
frightened Ferris was not the way in which the right arm was
extended and bent so that the hand, turned palm outward,
was close to the butt of the pistol in the loop of the waist
belt. The day of the fast-drawing gunfighter and his methods
was yet to come, so he had no conception what the posture
indicated.

It was the sheer magnetic driving force of Ole Devil's per-
sonality that produced the reaction!

Staring at him, the hardcase did not doubt for a single
instant that he was ready, willing, and completely able to kill
without mercy.

So the young Texian was, but he hoped that the necessity
would not arise!

Almost a minute dragged by on leaden feet, or so it
seemed to Ferris. Much as he hated to admit it even to himself, he did not dare attempt to pull out the knife although
he had no idea of how Ole Devil proposed to stop him. He
was aware that the only alternative was to back down and eat
crow. He could not hope for intervention on the part of the
other men. Although his main attention was riveted upon
the menacing figure confronting him, he was conscious of
the second male arrival's dispassionate gaze and sensed that

Hickert was also studying him, awaiting whatever came next with no great display of emotion.

Attracted by the commotion from their rear, Corrinne Hallistead and Maw Hickert had turned around. Neither of them knew exactly what had caused the trouble, but both suspected that it was not of Ole Devil's making. Knowing the hardcase, Maw had a solid basis for her belief. Corrinne had had considerable experience of men and had deduced correctly the natures of the protagonists in the little drama. So she felt sure that the young Texian had been provoked and guessed that he had no wish to take the matter further if it could be avoided.

Although the men had no intention of mediating, the same did not apply to the women. There was one difference in their attitudes. Maw had duplicated the little actress's conclusions but was unable to decide what would be the best way to ease the situation. Seeing Tommy Okasi approaching, Corrinne realized how she could achieve her purpose, at least as far as Ole Devil was concerned.

"Really, Maw!" the actress snorted, in tones of exasperation, starting to retrace her footsteps. "Isn't this just like *men*? There's poor little Tommy Okasi needing to be brought over the river, and they're playing foolish games."

"Danged if it don't make you want to give up on 'em," the big woman said, stepping out to catch up and keep pace with the other member of her sex. "Mose Hickert, you get them blasted oxen unhitched and turned around. And happen you're so all-fired eager to hear what that feller's got to say, you pair want to lend him a hand to do it."

"A most astute and commendable suggestion, my dear lady," Hallistead admitted, showing a trace of relief, as he realized what the women were hoping to do. "And one which I, with all promptitude, would advise that we apply ourselves to carrying out, Devil."

"I don't know what most of that was about," Maw growled. "But happen it means yes, get to it."

"With alacrity, although I am but slightly acquainted with

such a task," the entertainer assented. "Perhaps you would, having more experience possibly, care to instruct me, Devil."

"Why, sure," the Texian replied, but he did not turn away immediately. Instead, he addressed the hardcase in a quiet, matter-of-fact, yet somehow coldly threatening manner. "One thing, *hombre*. The Beaucoups have found out that I didn't kill Saul. So there'd be no bounty if you'd tried to claim it."

"Wha—" gasped Ferris, but Ole Devil had swung on his heel and was walking with Hallistead toward the oxen.

To give the hardcase his due, he had never heard of the reward offered by the Beaucoup family for Ole Devil's arrest and return. His animosity had arisen out of a sharecropper arrangement[3] he had made in Iberville Parish with Colonel Marsden Fog.

In spite of having been given several opportunities to change his ways, Ferris was always shiftless and idle, and his continued failure to uphold his end of the bargain had caused him to be evicted. As a result, his long-suffering wife had deserted him, and he had drifted to Texas in search of a way of earning a living that was not burdened with the need to do much work. When he had failed to achieve his goal, never being one to admit he was at fault, he had put the blame on the owner of the property he had been mismanaging. Brooding over it, he had extended his hatred to the whole of the Hardin, Fog, and Blaze clan. Ole Devil was the first of them with whom he had come into contact, and that alone was the reason why he had picked the fight.

Although Ferris did not realize it, he had had a very narrow escape. Many a man, especially when laboring under the strains that Ole Devil was enduring while at the same time possessing such effective fighting techniques, would not have thought twice about killing him.

Watching the straight-backed young Texian striding away,

3. Sharecropper: a tenant farmer who contracts to pay a share of his produce as his rent instead of money.

the hardcase muttered under his breath. Fear and resentment warred with each other inside him. The latter emotion cried for revenge, but the former cautioned against trying to obtain it. For once in his worthless life, he was ready to listen to the dictates of prudence and wisdom. That showed good sense. If he had offered to cause further trouble, Ole Devil could not have refrained from killing him.

"*Mr.* Ferris," Maw Hickert said as the hardcase started to rise.

"Yeah?" Ferris asked, looking over his shoulder.

"I hope you ain't fixing to make no more fuss for young Cap'n Hardin," the big woman went on, tapping the heavy oxgoad she was still holding against the palm of her left hand as if it weighed no more than a slender willow switch. " 'Cause *I* wouldn't like it if you do. Fact being, I reckon's you had a right smart notion when you was talking about pulling out and going to find General Sam 'n' enlist in the army. Why'n't you go and do it?"

"I reckon I will," Ferris replied, refusing to meet either woman's gaze. He knew better than to antagonize Maw and also was aware that she had never cared for him. So he doubted that he would be welcome to stay in Hickert's Landing even if the news that the little Oriental was bringing in such haste should—as was not likely—be favorable. "Yeah. I reckon I'll go and collect my gear 'n' head out now."

"Good luck to you," Maw grunted, then swung toward her bulky sons, who were hovering in the background. "Take care of them two hosses, Henry, and you see to that other when it gets across, Clyde. Come on, gal. I reckon's you and me can leave them shiftless menfolks to do the rest."

Oblivious of what had taken place behind them, but confident that one of the women would give a warning if the hardcase was contemplating further hostilities, Ole Devil and Hallistead, helped Hickert unhitch and turn the oxen. With the animals on the move, the Texian watched the boat creeping forward. As he did so, he began to think how useful it had been to travelers in the past and what an asset it would be if the struggle for independence were successful. However, it was also dangerous to the safety of the consignment if the enemy were allowed to capture and utilize it as a means of a rapid crossing of the San Bernard River.

"I'll be right sorry to lose this old boat, Cap'n," Hickert remarked, almost as if he were reading the Texian's mind.

"Yes, sir," Ole Devil answered. "But there's no way you could hold on to it if the Hopis are coming. Even if they passed you by, they'll want it should they come back with the consignment."

"That's for sure," Hickert admitted, then gave a fatalistic shrug. "Anyways, happen ole Santa Anna wins this fuss, which he could do a whole heap easier without General Sam having them caplocks, ain't no chance of him leaving us here to keep running her."

"You're right, sir," Ole Devil agreed. "He's sworn that he won't allow a single gringo to own land on Mexican soil in future. But if we win, your ferry will be needed more than ever."

"Likely," Hickert conceded, knowing that in all probability there would be an influx of colonists from the United States if the security of an independent republic could be attained. He darted a glance of curiosity at the younger man's satanic face. "Only *I* can't see's how we can have it both ways?"

"What do you have in mind, Devil?" Hallistead put in, having followed the conversation with interest and sharing the ferry owner's belief that the Texian was not merely making idle chatter.

"The Hopis would be willing to use the ferry," Ole Devil replied, watching the boat reach the western bank where Tommy was already waiting on the landing stage. "But because they come from Arizona, I don't think they would know how to refloat and repair it, even if they'd be willing to take the time."

"You're right!" Hallistead exclaimed, so impressed that he forgot to employ his usual verbose flow of words. "If the boat was sunk, trained men would be required to raise and repair it."

"Whoa!" Hickert bawled at the oxen, having been keeping the boat under observation. Realizing what the young Texian was driving at, he continued as soon as the order had been obeyed. "How about that bunch from San Patricio, could they do it?"

"From what I saw, there's a full brigade there," Hallistead answered as Ole Devil looked at him. "While I couldn't swear to their presence, my rudimentary knowledge of military organization leads me to suppose they have engineers accompanying them. However, as I mentioned while we were coming here, Devil, there was no sign of pursuit. Furthermore, all the reconnaissance activity which I observed in the, I admit, limited time they were subjected to my scrutiny was directed to the west. I would be inclined to suggest it will be in that direction, rather than northward, they are intending to devote their energies."

A faint grin flickered across the Texian's face as he watched Tommy leading the blue-roan gelding onto the boat. For all the entertainer's diffuse manner of speaking, he was no fool. What was more, in spite of his claim to know little about the subject, his conclusions on military matters were worth considering.

"You mean they'll go to Goliad to take care of Fannin's bunch afore they head out to join up with Santa Anna?" Hickert asked, remembering what Ole Devil had told him about the state of affairs elsewhere in Texas, and the fact that he directed the question at Hallistead showed he, too, accepted the entertainer was worth listening to.

"That would be my considered supposition, sir," Hallistead declared.

While talking, the three men had started to change the oxen.

"Santa Anna's sure to have engineers along, even if that bunch at San Patricio don't," Hickert guessed, stepping back after the completion of the work and setting the animals into motion. "I'd hate like hell for him to be able to use old Nellie there."

"It's not likely he'll come this far south," Ole Devil pointed out. "He'll be following General Houston, who's falling back toward Washington-on-the-Brazos and will go over thereabouts.[4] So they'll go by well to the north."

"What do you reckon'd be the best thing for us to do, Cap'n?" Hickert asked. "Sink her in midstream."

"That *would* be the safest way, sir," Ole Devil replied. "Or you could beach her somewhere downstream. Take out some of her bottom planks, load the cable onto one of your wagons, and drive the oxen along with you when you leave. I think that the Hopis will come after us, not you, so you'll be all right."

"Huh-huh!" Hickert grunted noncommittally, but he liked the solution he had been offered. Many a young man would not have troubled to think of such a thing. "How long do you conclude it'll be afore General Sam's ready for the showdown with 'em, Cap'n?"

"A month, or two at the most," Ole Devil decided, after a moment's thought. "He's falling back until he's certain our people are close enough to be able to escape over the U.S. line if things go badly."

"Was that all she'd be under, she wouldn't take no hurt," Hickert said quietly. "And happen we get run out, I'm such an ornery cuss that I'd sooner not have some Mexican taking her over unless he's had a heap of work to do."

"I'll leave how you handle it up to you, sir," Ole Devil stated, satisfied that he had achieved his purpose. "And of

4. Because of an inspired piece of trickery causing a change in both sides' strategy, the Texians finally crossed the Brazos River some miles south of Washington-on-the-Brazos, at what was then known as Groce's Place, on April 12 and 13, 1836. Having captured two canoes and a flatboat at Thompson's Ferry—which later became the town of Richmond, seat of Fort Bend County, Texas—the Mexicans went over on April 14, paving the way for the final battle. Further details of how all this came about and the result are given in *Ole Devil at San Jacinto*.

course, there might not be any need for you to do anything at all."

Even as he was speaking, Ole Devil and the other two men were looking at the approaching boat. Studying the condition of the little Oriental and his horse, the coat of which was white with lather to such an extent that its true color was almost completely hidden, they all realized the Texian was raising a false hope. Tommy would have driven his mount to such a state only if the matter were extremely urgent. There was no chance of the Hopis' having given up the pursuit. In fact, from all appearances, they could be very close at hand.

13
IF I CAN ASK THEM TO DIE, I CAN ASK YOU TO LIVE

Sitting with his back propped against a rock and fighting to stave off the tiredness that threatened to make him fall asleep, Ole Devil Hardin was once again waiting for Tommy Okasi to catch up and deliver a report. He hoped, but did not expect, that it would be one that would relieve his anxiety over the safety of the consignment. From what the little Oriental had told him on the previous occasion, he knew that he had at least bought himself a respite by his activities at Hickert's Landing, but he doubted whether he had seen the last of the Arizona Hopi Activos Regiment.

Taking sufficient time only for a drink of water and to compose himself on leaving the ferryboat, Tommy had told of his activities since parting company from his employer. One important point had been his suspicion that the Mexican officer with whom they had originally been in contact appeared to have assumed command of the regiment following the death of its previous colonel. If that was the case, unless Ole Devil was mistaken, he would be more determined than any of his fellow officers to continue the pursuit and have a reckoning with them.

Having seen the party of braves setting off, while the remainder of the regiment was making preparations to march, Tommy had guessed their purpose. Returning to his horse, he had ridden in the direction from which he had come. Smaller, lighter, and better mounted than any of the men he was seeking to avoid, he had increased his lead over them, and to the best of his knowledge, his presence ahead had not been discovered by the time he was at the river in the woodland.

Although, Tommy said, he had considered trying to delay the scouting party at the crossing, he had decided against putting his idea into effect. Prudence had dictated this decision. His supply of arrows was rapidly diminishing. While he had retrieved the shaft that had ruined the Hopi's bow and could use it again, the second that he had discharged had disappeared into the woodland, and he could not delay moving on to search for it. Nor was there any other way in which he could obtain a fresh supply until he had rejoined the main body of the Texas Light Cavalry and replenished his quiver from the stock he had left with the baggage train. Since his own were forty inches in length and had points peculiar to Japanese archery[1] to influence their weight and balance, he could not substitute them with the shorter and, in his opinion, vastly inferior arrows in both construction and utility which he could have taken from the dead warriors at Santa Cristóbal Bay.

As an added inducement to caution, the little Oriental had realized that his employer must be informed as quickly as possible that the enemy were so close and in much greater strength than had been anticipated. With that in mind, he had continued to travel at the best speed his mount could

1. Details of the special Japanese archery points and their use is given in *Ole Devil at San Jacinto.*

produce. The big blue-roan gelding had *brío escondido*[2] and needed it to cover the miles separating him from his destination.

Shortly before reaching Hickert's Landing, Tommy had climbed to the top of a hill. Searching his back trail with the aid of the telescope, he had not seen the Hopis' advance party. That had meant they were at least three miles away.

Accepting the little Oriental's summation, Moses Hickert had set about making preparations for departure. However, at his suggestion, Ole Devil had not waited until the work was completed. Leaving the owner and his family to carry out what they hoped was only the temporary disablement of the ferry, he had set off to rejoin the mule train. Fortunately they had had sufficient saddle horses to supply Tommy, Mangrove Hallistead, and himself with fresh mounts. The entertainer had offered his services in the defense of the consignment, but Ole Devil had convinced him that he would be better employed in ensuring that Major General Samuel Houston was informed of what had happened at San Patricio. So he was to accompany the Hickerts, with his wife riding in one of their wagons, when they set off to the northwest in search of the Republic of Texas's army. Tommy had also stayed behind, so that he could get some badly needed rest and keep watch at the San Bernard River.

Traveling hard, in spite of the fatigue that assailed him, Ole Devil had taken only sufficient pauses to allow his three-horse relay—two from the Hickerts and his linebacked dun gelding, which he had not ridden—to rest. He had caught up with the mule train shortly before noon that day. After telling Diamond Hitch Brindley, Sergeant Smith, and Joe Galton of the latest developments, he had sent Tom Wolf—who had returned from a successful visit to San Felipe—and three more of the Tejas Indian scouts to relieve the little Oriental. That had been three hours ago. Now, having rid-

2. *Brío escondido:* "hidden vigor," stamina, and endurance of an exceptional standard.

den one of his borrowed horses into the ground and reduced the second to a state of near exhaustion, Tommy was coming to where the Texian was waiting. The tidings he brought were a mixture of good and bad.

Shortly before night had fallen, the Hopis' advance party had come into sight of Hickert's Landing. However, by that time the owner and his sons had taken and sunk the boat in the middle of the river. Although they had still been removing the cable, having no firearms, the braves had not attempted to interfere in any way. The Hickerts and the Hallisteads had taken their departure in the darkness, but the warriors had not offered to try to cross the river. Instead, they had waited on the western bank until the rest of their regiment arrived the following morning.

Once he had come on the scene, the self-appointed Colonel Abrahán Felipe Gonzáles de Villena y Danvila had wasted no time in setting about the task of going over the water. For all that, there had been a considerable delay before his regiment could accomplish the crossing. Watched by Tommy from a distance, a party had swum to the eastern bank and, using timber wrested from the buildings, had started to construct rafts. However, once over, they had followed the consignment and ignored the tracks of the Hickerts' small party.

"They're after us," the little Oriental finished, looking at his audience of Ole Devil, Di, Smith, and Galton. "And they coming faster than the mules are moving."

"That figures, with Villena in command," the Texian replied. "A man like him won't easily forget, or forgive, us for making him leave his sword when he ran away."

"What'll we do, Devil?" Di asked. "The Brazos's only a couple of miles on, but I don't see how we can get across it hereabouts. There's no timber for us to make rafts and float the consignment over, and she's sure's hell too deep and wide to take it across on the mules."

"There isn't any chance of finding a boat we could use?"

Ole Devil asked, although he could guess what the answer was going to be.

"Not's I know of," the girl replied. "We could maybe go and take a look."

"That's what we'll do," Ole Devil agreed, getting to his feet. "You'd best come with me, Sergeant Smith."

"Yo!" the noncom answered.

"And you, if you will, Di," Ole Devil continued.

"Sure," the girl assented.

Tired as he was, the young Texian knew that there was an urgent need to survey the situation, and he was the one best equipped to carry it out. They had no hope of outrunning their pursuers. Nor could they reach safety before being overtaken. So unless they could find some means of crossing the Brazos River, they would have no choice but to stop and fight. If that was the only choice, he wanted to select the best place for them to do it.

The mule train had been kept moving while the council of war had taken place. Catching up with it, Ole Devil left Galton in charge and pushed on with Di, Tommy, and Smith. Studying the terrain as they were riding along, he concluded that the girl was correct. Although there were a few scattered trees, he could not see sufficient for them to be able to make rafts. However, on reaching the river, he decided that luck had not entirely deserted them.

The river having passed through a deep gorge, some freak of nature caused it on merging to make a U-shaped bend to the east, forming a sizable basin of land on the inside of the curve. There was a high and sheer cliff at the upstream arm of the U and steeply sloping, rocky, but otherwise fairly open ground on the lower side, over which horses could gallop only with great difficulty and at considerable risk to their riders.

Gazing around, Ole Devil knew that no body of horsemen as large as the seven companies of the Arizona Hopi Activos Regiment would be able to come closer than half a mile from the edge of the river without being detected. Furthermore, any mass attack down the sole means of easy access would have to be launched from a front slightly less than five hundred yards in width.

Against those advantages, there was only scanty natural cover for the defenders, and the hard, rocky nature of the soil at the bottom of the basin, where they must take up their position, precluded the digging of other than very shallow rifle pits. In addition, unlike on the previous occasion when they had fought against the Hopis, not only was the size of their force drastically reduced, but they would not have any element of surprise in their favor. Sufficient of the former attackers had survived and rejoined their companions to prevent a similar mistake from being made. They would have been warned that the tactics upon which they had relied had failed because of the unexpected ability of the proposed victims' weapons to fire in what should have been adverse or at least unfavorable weather conditions.

Although there had been and might still be one possibility of salvation for the consignment, he did not intend to rely upon its materializing. He decided that more in hope than expectancy, he would ask Tom Wolf—if the chief returned in time—or Di for permission to send one of the Tejas scouts in each direction to seek and bring it to him if it should be available.

"You've been along here before, haven't you, Di?" Ole Devil inquired, after he had explained the good and bad points of the hollow.

"More'n once," the girl admitted.

"Is there anywhere else that would be better that we could reach before the Hopis catch us?" Smith asked, guessing what his superior was considering.

"Nope, not's comes to mind offhand," Di decided, having screwed up her pretty face in concentration and visualized what she could remember of that particular section of the Brazos River. "There's nothing but open and level ground both ways from here on for maybe two days' travel."

"They'll be on to us before then," Ole Devil warned, and

glanced into the hollow. "So *this*'s where we make our stand. Let's go back and bring the train up."

"Shucks!" The girl sniffed, studying the Texian's and the little Oriental's haggard and tired faces. "Ain't no call for us all going. I reckon Smithie 'n' me can tend to that. You pair stay here and rest up until we get back."

"You do that, Tommy," Ole Devil began.

"And *you*, damn it!" Di injected.

"If I stop and sit down, I'm likely to fall asleep," Ole Devil protested. "And there's too much to be done before I can let that happen."

"All right then," the girl answered, with an air of brooking no interference or refusal, but realizing that she had heard the truth. "You head back, Smithie. I'll stop here 'n' help you keep awake, Devil."

"Sure, Di," the sergeant agreed, for once not looking to his superior for guidance. "Have you any orders before I go, sir?"

"Only one," Ole Devil replied, noticing that the noncom had said "before I go" instead of asking if he could leave, but making no comment or protest. Knowing that the other was acting with his best interests at heart, he decided it was not the time to stand on the formalities that should be due to his rank. Having received permission from Di to use the scouts as he had envisaged, he went on, "And *gracias*, the pair of you."

"*Es nada,*" Di drawled. "I'm used to having to talk sense to fool menfolks." Her gaze swung to Tommy, and she continued, "And here's an old 'n' wise Texian saying's *I've* just now made up. A feller's looks as dad-blasted tired's you do'd best get down and take some rest afore he falls down."

"Now I *know* it's time for me to brave the shogun's[3] wrath and go home," the little Oriental informed his employer.

---

3. Shogun: the hereditary commander in chief of the Japanese Army until the post was rescinded in 1868. Corrupted by foreigners to tycoon, the name added another word to the English language.

"Get some rest afore you go," the girl advised, apparently unmoved by the baleful glance at her that had accompanied Tommy's words. "If you don't, you'll never make it."

"She's right, amigo, much as I hate to have to say it," Ole Devil went on. "Go and have some sleep. I wish I could."

"How'd you fix to handle things, Devil?" Di asked, watching the slump-shouldered and swaying little Oriental riding away and realizing just how close to complete exhaustion he must be. If anything, his exertions recently had been even greater than those of his employer.

"Like I said, make a stand on the banks down there," the Texian replied, speaking slowly as he struggled to remain awake and thinking. "We'll make the Hopis suffer the heaviest casualties possible and still stop them from taking the consignment."

"How do you figure on doing that, take it across the river?"

"I doubt if there's any way we could do that in the time. Nor is there much chance of our moving the ammunition over without its getting ruined by the water. Even if we did, with the hatred he has for us, Villena would keep after us. No. I intend to stop him here— Or make him believe there's no point in continuing the pursuit."

"How?" Di demanded.

"As soon as the mules get here, I want you to have them unloaded and moved across the river," Ole Devil explained, being aware that at least one of his subsequent proposals was going to meet with considerable opposition when the girl heard it but equally determined it would be carried out. "We'll move over as many of the caplocks as we can. They'll not take any harm if they get wet, greased up as they are. I'll keep, say, four loaded and ready to be used for every man who volunteers to stay with me—"

"Volunteers?" Di repeated.

"There'll be no way that anybody who stays with me can escape," Ole Devil elaborated. "I won't order my men to do it on those terms."

"If I know them, there's not one who'll say no," Di stated.

"It will be their choice," Ole Devil replied, and felt sure that the girl was correct in her assumption. "We'll stack up all the remaining ammunition behind our positions and cover it with a tarpaulin so that it looks as if the whole consignment's there ready to be taken."

"Only it'll be fixed so's they can't lay their cotton-picking hands on it happen they whup us," Di guessed, although because she had already seen several examples of the young Texian's skill at making plans to take care of possible contingencies, the words came out more as a statement.

"There'll be a powder flask in the middle, with a piece of quick match fixed down its nozzle and taken to the back of the pile," Ole Devil confirmed. "When there's no further hope of holding them off, Sergeant Smith will set fire to it and take some more of them with us."

"There's some's might say that's a real sneaky trick to pull on them poor Injuns," Di commented dryly, but she was even more impressed by the further evidence of her companion's forethought. Realizing that the need might arise to prevent the consignment from falling into the wrong hands, he had the presence of mind to procure a length of quick match[4] fuse cord from General Houston's headquarters and carry it with him. "We'll sure teach them varmints a lesson they'll not soon forget."

"Yes," Ole Devil agreed, and he dismounted, ready for the storm which he knew would soon be breaking. "You can count on my men and me to do that."

Swinging from her saddle, so as to join the Texian on the ground, Di suddenly realized how his comment had been worded.

"What's all this about you and your men?" the girl asked grimly, stepping to confront the young man. "Just where in

4. Quick match: a cord impregnated with black powder to produce an exceptionally fast-burning fuse for igniting flares, fireworks, and explosive charges.

hell do you reckon me 'n' my boys'll be at while you're doing it?"

"Across the river, with the mules," Ole Devil replied.

"Like hell we will!" Di blazed. "If you reckon we're going to sit on our butts over there while you and those boys of yourn're getting killed—"

"That's the way it has to be," Ole Devil said, seeming to grow calmer as the girl became more heated and indignant.

"If you think because I'm a woman—" Di burst out.

"That's got nothing to do with it," Ole Devil interrupted, placing his hands on her shoulders. "And you know it."

"God damn it, Devil!" Di almost shouted, feeling his grasp tighten slightly as she tried to step away. Seeing the tension on his face, she refrained from continuing the attempt, and her voice became milder as she went on. "You can't ask *me* to leave you and your boys— Not with what you're asking *them* to do."

"You're wrong, Di," Ole Devil contradicted, but gently, looking straight into her eyes. "If I can ask them to die, I can ask you to live."

"But—" the girl began, wishing she could turn her head and avoid his disconcerting gaze.

"My men and I are soldiers," Ole Devil went on. "It's our duty to fight and, if need be, get killed—"

"You let me side them at the top of Santa Cristóbal Bay," the girl protested, but with far less vehemence than previously.

"That was to shame the dragoons into doing things the way I wanted," Ole Devil pointed out, and his voice took on a slightly harder edge. "I'd not take kindly to you thinking *my men* needed *that* sort of inducement to make them fight."

"Such a thought never entered my head!" Di objected indignantly. "Those boys of yourn—"

"Will do their duty," Ole Devil finished for her, resuming his previous almost emotionless drawl. "And I'm counting on *you* to do yours."

"Then let—"

"Even if you didn't have to deliver all the caplocks we can get across the river to General Houston, those trained packers and mules are too valuable to him for you to lose them here."

"But with me and my boys helping you—" the girl commenced hopefully.

"The result would be just the same," Ole Devil interrupted, and took his hands from her shoulders. Glancing down the slope, he found that Tommy was already lying on the ground, wrapped in a blanket, and, using his saddle for a pillow, asleep. "I'm not selling your men short as fighters, Di. With them at our side, we'll delay and kill more of the Hopis, but the rest will swamp us under by sheer weight of numbers. Believe me, I don't want to do it this way. But there's no other. So will you do as I'm asking—please?"

For several seconds the girl did not reply. Instead, she first stared long and hard at the satanic features she had come to know so well. She had the same high regard for Ole Devil as she had for her grandfather and Joe Galton, but acceding to his request did not come easily. With a long and heartfelt sigh, she swung her gaze to the approaching mule train. As before, the cavalrymen were bringing up the rear. From the beginning they had treated her with an easygoing respect that neither ignored nor played upon her sex. Leaving them to fight and almost certainly to die was not a thing she could contemplate lightly.

Although Ole Devil did not speak again after making the request, Di knew she must not delay with her reply. The mule train would have reached them in three more minutes, and there was little enough time to spare for all the work that must be carried out. What was more, unpalatable as the thought might be, she had to admit he was making good sense when he mentioned the value of the mules and their packers. Nor could she see any alternative action he might take to safeguard even a portion of the consignment.

"All right," Di said, her voice just a trifle hoarse. Then she made a not entirely unsuccessful attempt to resume the kind of banter she usually employed with the Texian. "There's only one thing, Ole Devil Hardin. Happen you go and get killed for being so cussed, I'll never speak to you again."

"I don't suppose you will," Ole Devil answered, also speaking more lightly than throughout the conversation. "Because where I'll be going, they'll never let *you* in."

14
THIS TIME THERE WON'T BE *ANY* MISTAKES

"And that's how it stands, gentlemen," Ole Devil Hardin warned, looking at the tanned faces of the remaining members of the company under his command. He knew every one of them, young, middle-aged, and old, and was all too aware of the immensity of the thing he would be asking them to do. "I want volunteers to stay with me."

Beyond the group of men who had been gathered around their commanding officer by Sergeant Smith, the bottom of the U-shaped basin formed by a curve in the Brazos River was alive with feverish, yet organized and purposeful activity. Working as quickly as they could under Joe Galton's supervision, Diamond Hitch Brindley's Tejas Indian mule packers were unloading their charges and stacking the caplock rifles separately from the boxes of ready-made paper cartridges and percussion caps. However, having explained to the *cargador* very briefly what needed to be done, the girl was leaving him to attend to it so that she could watch how the soldiers responded to their superior's request.

Having told Smith to leave the remaining Tejas scout to keep watch from the rim and assemble the remnants of

Company C at the foot of the slope, Ole Devil had seen to his linebacked dun gelding. Then, without attempting to belittle the danger or raising false hopes of the possibility of survival, he had told them how he was planning to deal with their desperate predicament. He had pointed out the importance of inflicting the greatest possible number of casualties on the Arizona Hopi Activos Regiment not only to enhance the chances of safety for the caplocks and mule train but to lessen their effectiveness as a fighting unit which could be thrown against the Republic of Texas's already greatly outnumbered army. He had also pointed out that in order to make sure no more loot than was absolutely necessary fell into their attackers' clutches, he would be sending all the company's horses across the river with the mules, and restrict the defenders' arms to, at the most, four extra rifles each from the consignment. And having told them all this, he waited to discover how they would respond to the call he was making upon them.

Standing a few feet away, Di clenched her hands until the knuckles showed white. She waited with bated breath to see how many of the men would do as Ole Devil asked.

Would any of them be willing to sacrifice themselves?

There was a scuffling of feet and an interplay of exchanged glances, but for several seconds—which seemed to drag on far longer to the watching girl—none of the soldiers spoke or moved from his position. It seemed that faced with making a decision, every one of them was waiting for somebody else to take the initiative.

Never had Di experienced such a sensation of suspense. It was all she could do to hold back from screaming a demand that some, *any*, response must be made.

At last there was a movement!

"Well now, Cap'n," drawled a white-haired and leathery featured old-timer, whose military service had commenced by fighting the British at the—as was subsequently proved unnecessary—Battle of New Orleans.[1] He advanced a pace. "One thing I promised meself when I left the good ole U.S. of A. was that I'd only volunteer just one more time in my wicked 'n' ornery life. Which same I done it when I joined the Texas Light Cavalry."

"Go on, Jube," Ole Devil prompted, wondering what was coming next.

"It be this way with me, Cap'n," the old-timer obliged, neither his expression nor the timbre of his voice supplying the slightest clue to his sentiments. "I'm knowed's a man of me word, 'mongst other things. So I can't speak for none of the others, mind, but the only way I'll stay—or *go*, comes to that—is if *you-all* up 'n' orders me to do it."

"What Jube means, Cap'n Hardin," Smith elaborated, stepping with military precision to the old-timer's side. "is happen you want us along, we'll stick here, root, hawg, or die."

"Shucks, I can't see's there's all that much for us to worry about," Sammy Cope went on cheerfully, aligning himself with the two previous speakers. "There might be a fair slew of 'em coming, but they ain't but Mexicans 'n' house Injuns."[2]

"Damn it, yes," another of the enlisted men continued. "Was they Comanch' it'd be some different, dangerous even. But *this* bunch—well, blast it, we've close to got 'em outnumbered."

1. The Battle of New Orleans: The final engagement of the War of 1812, fought on January 8, 1815, ended in a decisive victory for the United States. At a loss of seventy-one casualties, the Americans killed almost two thousand troops, including Major General Sir Edward Pakenham, who had commanded the ill-fated expedition. This is an even more glaring example than is given in footnote 1 on page 62 of the effect of slow communications. Peace had been signed in Ghent, Belgium, fifteen days earlier, but the news of this had not been received by the combatants.
2. House Indians: Unlike the nomadic, hunting, and raiding tribes, the predominantly pastoral and agriculturalist Hopi, Zuñi, and kindred nations tended to build and live in permanent houses instead of using transportable lodges and tepees.

"Bad luck, Cap'n," Smith said with a grin. "It looks like you haven't got rid of this worthless bunch. So, happen you tell me what you want done, I'll set 'em to doing it for you."

"*Gracias*, gentlemen," Ole Devil stated, his voice husky as he fought to keep from showing his emotions.

"Danged if I can ever ree-member being called *that* afore." Jube grinned. "And I don't conclude's how I'll ever get called it ag'in."

"You'll get called something more apt happen you keep butting in when the cap'n's trying to tell us something," Smith warned the old-timer.

Utilizing the brief respite gained by the two men's comments to regain his composure, Ole Devil stiffened as well as his tired condition would allow. They had won a few hours' grace by the destruction of the ferry at Hickert's Landing. So it must be utilized to the best possible advantage. Forcing his weary brain to function, he began to formulate the arrangements which would allow the defenders to inflict the greatest damage on their assailants before the inevitable conclusion. Having done so, he made a change in his intentions with regard to the consignment. While Houston had powder and lead to make balls for the caplocks, the percussion caps were not a commodity readily available in Texas. So because they were less susceptible to damage by water than the paper cartridges would be, he asked Di to try to take them with her.

"I'll tend to it," the girl promised, and turned her gaze to the sergeant. "Hey, Smithie, do you ever get the feeling's how you could get along just fine once you've been told what to do and don't need somebody looking over your shoulder?"

"I've had it now and again," the noncom replied, guessing what Di had in mind. "Do you need Cap'n Hardin anymore?"

"*Me?*" the girl asked. "The hell I do. I've got more'n enough worthless and shiftless loafers on my hands now without taking another's looks like he's fixing to fall asleep on his feet."

"All right. *All right!*" Ole Devil sighed, but darted a look of gratitude at the two speakers. "Let it never be said that I can't take a hint. Have a couple of pickets posted on the rim, Ser—"

"With respect, sir," Smith interrupted politely, "I reckon if I didn't have enough sense to think *some* things out for myself, you'd never have made me a sergeant."

"You could be right at that," Ole Devil conceded. "So you can take command while I have some rest."

"Yo!" Smith responded. "And, again respectfully, sir, don't tell me to wake you if anything happens."

"Very well, Sergeant," Ole Devil promised with a wry grin. "I won't. But if you need me, I'll be over there with Tommy."

Collecting his blankets, the young Texian went to where the little Oriental was already deep in the arms of Morpheus.[3] After a final and quick look around, deciding that he could count on Smith to do everything necessary without further assistance on his part, he wrapped himself in his blankets and lay alongside his employee. Within seconds of his head's touching the saddle—which had already been taken from his dun by Galton's Indian assistant farrier—having covered his face with his hat, he had fallen into a deep, badly needed, and well-earned sleep. Nor did the work that was being carried on not too far away disturb his or Tommy's slumbers.

Leaving Smith to attend to the military side of their affairs, Di supervised the work being carried out by her men. Realizing just how much work had to be done, the noncom decided to use his initiative in regard to the posting of pickets. While explaining his strategy, Ole Devil had said that—as before the battle at Santa Cristóbal Bay—the Hopis' scouts could be allowed to see the arrangements being made

3. Morpheus: in Grecian mythology the son of Hypnos, god of sleep, and god of dreams in his own right.

for their regiment's reception. So Smith let the Tejas keep
watch and retained the services of two extra pairs of hands.

With the mules unloaded, the business of getting them to
the eastern bank of the Brazos was commenced. This was a
vastly different proposition from the crossing of the ford in
the woodland. There the distance had not been anywhere
near as great, and the water was much shallower. So the
mules, being unable to see the opposite shore, would be far
more reluctant to enter even with the inducement of following the bell mare. On top of that, there was the matter of
transporting over the rifles and boxes of percussion caps.

Bearing in mind all the experience she had gathered in the
years she had spent at the business of mule packing, Di knew
that while difficult, the latter task was not insurmountable.
The mules could not swim with the bulky loads but would be
able to carry five of the rifles on each side of their *aparejo*,
the whole being covered by tarpaulin and roped into position. She had brought along fifty mules, excluding the animals assigned to carry the cook's and farrier's equipment,
which meant she had sufficient for her needs. However, the
supply of grain would have to be left behind, and she ordered that it was to be placed with the ammunition. Not only
would it help convey the impression that the full consignment had been abandoned, but the subsequent explosion
would ensure that it was lost to the Hopis as well as to her.

Sharing his superior's conclusion about the unsuitability of
the ground for digging adequate rifle pits, Smith assigned
only half his men to that job. The rest were to help break
down the bundles of caplocks or stack the ammunition and
sacks of grain behind the defensive positions.

About half an hour later the Tejas scout on the rim attracted Di's attention. Joining him, accompanied by Smith,
she found that three Hopis had come into view. However,
they were still a good half mile away and keeping that distance. Nor was there sufficient cover for them to ride closer.
Telling her man to continue keeping them under observa-

tion, she and the noncom returned to the bottom of the basin.

Shortly after nightfall the crossing commenced. Going over in daylight would have been easier, but there were practical and tactical objections to this. Not the least was the discovery that while his three companions were holding the attention of the Tejas lookout, a fourth Hopi scout had slipped around and was studying the basin from the top of the sheer cliff on the upstream side. Instead of having him dislodged, Smith allowed him to carry out his scrutiny undisturbed.

There was a sound reason for the noncom's decision. The pastoral Hopis did not have the raiding tradition as highly developed as the more warlike nomadic Indian nations, but he believed a desire to gather booty rather than patriotic fervor had brought them to Texas. If they learned that the mule train and remuda had gone, they might insist on following instead of trying to capture the consignment. Nor could the evacuation of the animals be left until dawn, since this was the time their attack was most likely to be launched.

At Di's suggestion, the remuda was sent over first. Then the bell mare was led into the cold and uninviting water by Galton, who had removed and was carrying her bell's harness. As he swam, supported by holding his horse's saddle with one hand, he used the other to shake the bell and increase the volume of its sound. The mules set off after her, and some followed without needing urging. However, in the urgency of the situation, no stubborn refusals could be tolerated. Any animal trying to balk was roped around the neck and hauled in until it was compelled to swim. Once started in this fashion, the dissidents followed their more compliant companions.

On reaching the eastern bank, the remuda and the mules were kept moving to a hollow about half a mile away. It had been found earlier by Prays Loudly, Sometimes. In the absence of the regular scouts, he had been sent over to select a location in which they could bed down for the night and would be hidden from their enemies. Such was the high standard of the packers that in spite of the darkness, when the halt was called, each found and unloaded his five-strong string. However, there was still work to be done. Several of the remuda were still saddled, and these had to be sought out and attended to. In addition, a further crossing of the river was required to bring back the dismantled equipment of the carrier and cook. Lastly, some of the driftwood that had accumulated on the banks—none of which had been suitable for making rafts—was collected. A couple of fires were lit in the hollow, allowing Di and her men to dry their clothing and warm themselves. When all that was done, they settled down to await the coming of the fateful dawn.

* * *

Returning from their scouting mission, having located the camp of the Arizona Hopi Activos Regiment, Tom Wolf and his three companions heard the sound of horses coming toward them. When they stopped their own mounts, the fact that whoever was riding their way did not duplicate their actions suggested their presence had not been detected. A low hiss of annoyance left the chief's lips. The riders were not heading straight at them but would pass some distance off to the right. There was no cover of any consequence in that direction, and it would be impossible to go any closer on horseback—unlike the packers, he and his men did not use mules—without being located.

Tall, well made, exuding an aura of quiet dignity and strength, Tom Wolf was an impressive figure. In spite of wearing a white man's style of buckskins and a round-topped black hat with an eagle's feather in its band, he had all the majesty of a war leader belonging to one of the free-ranging Plains Indians' nations. Dressed in a similar fashion, his scouts also looked what they were: tough and hardy braves, competent at their duties and ready to give their best in battle.

Many colonists had small regard for the Tejas Indians as warriors. Nor, in general, did members of the nation deserve it. That did not apply to Ewart Brindley's employees. They belonged to a band that had never been subdued by the Mexicans or suffered exposure to the "civilizing" influence of the Spanish missions. What was more, the old man had shielded them from the more corrosive aspects of contact with much of the Anglo-Saxon population. So, instead of being dissolute and dissipated—the fate of most others of their tribe—they retained the best qualities of the Indian people.

Following their chief's example, the braves slipped from their horses and allowed the reins to dangle free. Easing back the hammer of the caplock rifle presented to him by Ole Devil Hardin for his services at the Battle of Santa Cristóbal Bay, he listened to the clicks which told him his men were taking the same precaution. However, there was nothing to suggest the other riders in the darkness had heard the sounds.

Leaving their horses ground hitched by the dangling reins, the Tejas party advanced. They crouched low, feeling out the ground ahead with their feet and doing all they could to avoid making any noise. Before long they could make out the shapes of the riders. The nearest, as they rode in single file, was about forty yards away.

"Four!" Wolf counted silently and started to raise his rifle knowing there was no hope of going closer than they now were without being seen.

There was, the chief realized as he aimed at the second rider, no way he could warn his companions of his intentions. However, they all were experienced warriors and would select the correct victims. So he must rely upon Jimmy-Whoop at his right to take the leading Hopi—which the quartet undoubtedly was, no doubt a scouting party who were returning from a similar mission to their own—while Eats Grasshoppers and Bad Breath respectively dealt with the third and fourth in line.

Making sure of his aim, Wolf squeezed the caplock's trigger. Even as the hammer began to descend, he was conscious

of the brief flicker of sparks as the flint struck and pushed
aside the frizzen of Jimmy-Whoop's rifle so they could fall
into the pan.[4] There was a whoosh and glow of flame as the
priming powder ignited, mingling with the slight pop of the
exploding percussion cap and deeper crack from the main
charge in the breech of the caplock as it was detonated.
Almost simultaneously, a similar reaction on the other side
of the chief informed him that the men there had touched
off their flintlocks.

Although Eats Grasshoppers' and Bad Breath's rifles vomited out their loads like echoes to Wolf's shot, Jimmy-
Whoop's weapon misfired. Except for the flash in the pan,
there was no discharge from it.

With that exception, the Tejas's impromptu volley was successful. Dazzled by the glare of the muzzle blasts from their
firearms, none of them was able to see Wolf's and Eats
Grasshoppers' victims struck and knocked from the horses.
Letting out a screech of pain as Bad Breath's bullet tore into
him, the fourth rider was in no condition to cope with the
behavior of his startled mount. As it made a bounding
plunge and bolted, he was pitched from its back.

Unscathed, because of the failure of Jimmy-Whoop's rifle,
the leading Hopi was able to avoid being dislodged when his
mount displayed a similar alarm to that shown by its companions. Retaining his seat as it started a bucking run to get
away from the commotion, he did not attempt to slow the
animal down. In fact, being able to guess who had attacked
his party—although uncertain of how many of the enemy
were involved—he was determined to make good his escape
and deliver the information he had collected.

Allowing a good two miles to fall behind him before he
brought his horse to a halt, the Hopi paused for long enough
to satisfy himself that he was not being followed. Deciding

4. Ole Devil Hardin could not present all the scouts with caplock rifles as,
in their eyes, this would have lessened the honor and respect he was
paying to the chief by making the gift.

that none of his companions had escaped and he was not being pursued by any of their assailants, he set the animal into motion and directed it toward the red glow in the sky which marked the site of his regiment's camp.

Half an hour later the surviving scout was standing in the presence of the Mexican officers and his fellow Hopi chiefs. Although he had deserted his companions, he made no attempt to hide or excuse his actions. They had been on a reconnaissance, not a raiding or fighting, mission. So it had been his duty to save himself and report his findings to his superiors, not to try to avenge or rescue those who had fallen in the ambush.

Freshly awakened, "Colonel" Abrahán Felipe Gonzáles de Villena y Danvila stood scowling and huddled against the chill of the night in the blankets which had formed his bed. Before he had heard many of the newcomer's words, he lost all of his resentment over having had his sleep disturbed.

Using the point of his knife to draw an accurate map of the area in which their quarry was located, employing a piece of bare ground for the purpose, the scout delivered a thorough description of their activities.

"So you think they've taken at least the majority of the rifles across the river, Chief?" asked Major Santoval, at the conclusion of the report.

"*Sí*, señor," the scout replied. "They took off the loads, but not the saddles, and I saw them fastening on rifles as the light was fading."

"But you think some of them will be staying on this side?" Villena inquired, darting a malevolent scowl at the commanding officer of Company Five for having anticipated his question.

"*Sí*, señor," the scout agreed. "They made a pile with many small, square boxes and sacks of grain. And the palefaces were digging the kind of holes from which they fought us the last time. They also sent more men to help the Indian who watched from the top of the hollow."

"That means they'll be waiting for us," guessed the sycophantic Major Méndez-Castillo, who commanded Company Eight, guessing his superior would welcome such a comment.

"Or want us to think they are," Santoval pointed out, "when they've all crossed and are marching through the night."

"They're waiting!" Villena stated. "The boxes will contain ammunition, which, as they've no boats, they can't take over without its being ruined by the water. And if I know that damned Texian, he won't leave it for us. So we'll go get it in the morning. And this time, there won't be any mistakes."

Listening to the plan that their self-appointed "colonel" was outlining, not even the normally critical Major Santoval could find a fault with it. If they carried out the plan the way Villena intended, they not only would deal with whoever was waiting but could resume their pursuit of the mule train and capture the rifles it was transporting.

15

THERE WILL BE *NO* QUARTER

"Well, it won't be long now," Sergeant Smith said quietly as he stood with Ole Devil Hardin, Tommy Okasi, and Tom Wolf in the center of the Texas Light Cavalry detachment's all too small defensive perimeter and looked at the rim of the basin. "I reckon it's too late now to start wishing I'd lived a better life."

"This's the kind of time when most folks get to thinking it," Ole Devil replied, without taking his attention from the sight which was holding all their interest. "But at least they're playing the way we want and haven't passed us by to go after the mule train."

"The scout we took alive said their Mexican leader had a great hatred for you, *Diablo Viejo*," Wolf remarked, speaking English for once. "And that it was a desire to take revenge on you that made him keep after you when others wanted to turn back."

Although fluent in their tongue, unless he respected the white men he was addressing, the chief of the Tejas Indians employed by Ewart Brindley would usually speak in either Spanish or his own language.[1]

After interrogating the dying scout, Wolf had sent two of his men to tell Ole Devil what they had seen and done so far. Accompanied by the third, he had returned to where they had already seen the Arizona Hopi Activos Regiment making camp. Leaving Bad Breath to take care of their horses, he had gone forward on foot. Although he had been successful in penetrating the ring of pickets, the Hopis had picked a site for their camp which would not allow a surprise attack against them to succeed. Nor was there any way he could get close enough to their horse lines to try to delay the pursuit by scattering the animals.

Watching from as close as he could reach while still remaining undetected, the chief had not been able to hear what was said by the surviving Hopi scout to the assembled Mexican officers and Indian war leaders. However, he had deduced that the man had succeeded in studying Ole Devil's defensive arrangements and a plan of campaign was being made. Then the Hopis had aroused their men and commenced making what he assumed to be their war medicine. Shortly before sunup a group of braves about twenty strong had made ready to leave. Concluding that they were to be an advance scouting party, which would be followed at a more leisurely pace—to conserve the horses' energy for the assault—by the rest of the regiment, he had withdrawn.

Traveling fast, Wolf and Bad Breath had found the small

1. This is a trait shared by warrant and noncommissioned officers who served in the now-disbanded Kings African Rifles regiments. One with whom I worked for several months during the Mau Mau uprising in Kenya had been to England and taken the drill instructors' course at the Brigade of Guards Depot, Pirbright, Surrey, shortly after World War II, during which he had served with distinction in, among other places, Burma. Although he could understand verbal instructions and read in English, it was only with reluctance that he would speak anything other than his tribal language, Wakamba, or the simplified form of Swahili that was the lingua franca of East Africa. J. T. E.

defending force awake and in position when they arrived at the basin. Without satisfying his curiosity over the absence of the mule train, having, in fact, made an accurate guess at why it had been sent away, he had informed Ole Devil of what he had seen and been told. Knowing him to be a man of shrewd judgment, the Texian had accepted his summation of the situation. Ole Devil had also accepted his offer that he and the other scouts remain instead of going after their employer. With the assurance that he could return, Eats Grasshoppers had taken his companions' horses across the river. Wanting to prevent such a valuable item as the Browning slide repeating rifle from being taken by the enemy, Ole Devil had sent it and the pouch of reserve magazines with the scout, retaining his two pistols and the bowie knife with which to do his share of the fighting.

With all the preparations made, there had been nothing for the defenders to do except wait. Yet that had been the hardest part of all for them. Every one had appreciated what a desperate situation they were facing. They might each have four loaded firearms available—with the exception of Tommy Okasi, who preferred to depend upon his samurai's weapons—but even with the addition of the Tejas scouts they would be outnumbered by almost ten to one. If the Hopis pressed home a charge with sufficient determination—and none of them expected otherwise—they were sure to swamp all resistance by the sheer weight of their numbers.

Although Wolf had stated that from what he had seen while returning, the attack would not happen for some time, none of the defenders could relax. In fact, it had almost been a relief when Jube—who was in command of the pickets on the rim—reported that the Hopis' advance party was in view. Following their orders, the eight men had fallen back to their companions without offering to resist. Shortly after, the braves had appeared at the top of the slope. Holding a brief consultation, they had obviously decided that the Texians were too strong for them to tackle unaided. So, apart from a warrior who had been sent to inform their superiors, they had done no more than keep the basin under surveillance. Almost an hour later a Mexican officer had joined them. He had studied the defensive positions and scanned the opposite side of the river through a telescope, probably trying to locate the mule train, then departed to inform his superiors of the situation. Yet another ninety minutes had dragged by before the rumble of many hooves had heralded the arrival of the main body.

"Then he will soon have his chance to get revenge," Ole Devil declared, watching the numbers of the enemy increasing until they formed an almost solid mass across the front down which they would be moving if they wanted to ride into the attack.

"Very soon, I would say," Wolf replied, gripping the caplock rifle appreciatively and glancing around. "Ah, *Diablo Viejo*, this will be a remembered fight."

"It's an honor to have you at our side, Chief," the Texian replied.

"My thanks," Wolf said quietly but sincerely. Then he raised his voice and addressed the rest of the defenders with the traditional exhortation of a war leader who knew that a hard battle would soon commence. "Brave up, brothers. This is a good day to die."

Almost as if to challenge the chief's inspiring and defiant words, the martial notes of a bugle rang out from the top of the slope. Listening to them, every member of the pitifully small defending force took a firmer grasp on the weapon he was holding and looked upward.

As the sound died away, there was a movement among the massed ranks that were sitting their horses on the rim!

Even before the bugle call had ended, Ole Devil became aware that he was not hearing the Mexican Army's usual signal for a charge. However, knowing that the Arizona Hopi Activos Regiment was made up of privately recruited and equipped volunteers, he considered it likely that it had instituted its own system of passing commands in such a manner.

Yet there was no concerted advance when the bugle ceased to blow!

Instead, only one Mexican officer and a single Hopi brave, the latter carrying a lance with something white flapping from its head, rode forward.

"Hold your fire, men!" the young Texian called, realizing what was happening, although he was puzzled by the development.

Over the centuries, in Europe particularly, a conventional means of requesting a parley had been formulated and generally accepted. It had been brought to the New World in the course of colonization by members of various nations to whom it was known. First calls from a bugle gave notice that no surprise was intended. Then the displaying of a white flag announced a desire for a truce and conversation.

Studying the approaching pair, Ole Devil was disturbed. The Mexican was in his early thirties, and his formerly well-fleshed figure had lost considerable weight since he had been fitted for his uniform. There was a wary expression on his face, which showed signs of his recent exertion, but that was understandable under the circumstances. However, he showed that he had a sound knowledge of the procedure for calling a parley.

"Good morning, gentlemen." The Mexican greeted them in good English, halting about thirty yards away from the nearest rifle pit. "I am Major Ramón Méndez-Castillo, commanding Company Eight of the Arizona Hopi Activos Regiment, and I speak with the authority of Colonel Abrahán Felipe Gonzáles de Villena y Danvila."

"Good morning, Major," Ole Devil replied, meeting politeness with politeness. "I am Captain Jackson Baines Hardin, commanding Company C, Texas Light Cavalry."

"Colonel Villena is a humane man, and he has no wish to shed blood unnecessarily, gentlemen. So he has sent you this ultimatum," Méndez-Castillo went on, studying the grim faces of the defenders and deciding there was no point in extending the formalities. "If you lay down your arms and give your parole to leave Mexican territory immediately, you will be permitted to do so. If you refuse, he will—with great reluctance—be compelled to order an attack. In that event, no prisoners will be taken, and there will be no quarter given."

"My thanks to Colonel Villena for his consideration, Major," Ole Devil answered, without glancing to see how the offer might be affecting his companions. "And assure him that I regard his word as being as binding as that of General Cós." He saw Méndez-Castillo's fleshy lips tighten and knew that his meaning was understood,[2] so continued. "And will you also tell him that I too am a humane man? So I will send him *my* terms. If he will order his men to lay down their arms and *surrender* to *us*, we will take a chance and accept *his* parole to leave the Republic of Texas and take no further military action within its boundaries."

A scowl creased the Mexican officer's surly features as the Texians chuckled at their superior's counterproposal. However, guessing why it had been made, he retained control of his temper. He was helped in this by knowing that Villena had never expected the offer to be accepted and, in fact, had made plans which would be carried out whether it was or not. Realizing that his work was not yet ended, he went on with it.

"You have no chance, not even the slightest, of survival, gentlemen," Méndez-Castillo warned, hating to use the honorific but willing to do so if it served to bring about his superior's wishes. He was directing the words at the defenders rather than to their leader. "Why throw your lives away on such a futile venture when you can leave in safety?"

2. On December 6, 1835, at the end of a battle lasting for six days, General Martín Perfecto de Cós—brother-in-law of Presidente Antonio López de Santa Anna—and his force of eleven hundred men had surrendered to the Texians at San Antonio de Béxar. Although Cós had accepted similar terms to those Ole Devil Hardin had been offered by Major Méndez-Castillo, he had broken his parole and was accompanying the Mexican Army which *el presidente* was leading to crush the rebellion.

"Shall I shoot him now, Cap'n Hardin?" Jube inquired in a matter-of-fact tone. "Or do I have to wait until he comes back with his men?"

"I'll have you court-martialed if you shoot him while he's here under a flag of truce, blast it!" Ole Devil declared, noticing that alarm had replaced the somewhat smug condescension with which the Mexican had been watching them. He felt himself grow increasingly perturbed but did not show it and continued, keeping his unwavering gaze fixed upon Méndez-Castillo's face. "You have had *my* answer, Major. And I think that I had better point out your flag does not give you the right to try to seduce my men from their duty."

That might, the young Texian realized, be the real reason behind the request for a parley. Yet he could not convince himself it was anything so simple.

No matter what else Villena might be, he was no fool. He would realize that there was little chance of persuading the defenders to surrender on such terms. Even before news of Cós's perfidy had become known, the Anglo-Saxon colonists had learned to be very wary of Mexican promises.

So why had Méndez-Castillo been sent on such an errand? There had to be some other, more definite reason!

Finding out went far beyond merely satisfying curiosity!

It could be a matter of life or death!

Everything about the Mexican's bearing and attitude struck Ole Devil as being wrong. Partly it was suggestive of a man who held a royal straight flush[3] at stud poker when the upcards[4] proved no other could be out and he would not fail to win the pot. Yet there was also something furtive, nervous even, about him as if he considered that he was in, or very close to, some serious danger.

3. Royal straight flush: Ace, king, queen, jack, and ten all of the same suit.
4. Upcards: In stud poker, each player's first or hole card is dealt facedown, and the remainder—usually four, but there can be more depending upon the variation being played—are exposed.

Had the latter sentiment been in evidence before Jube had injected his comment?

Did the Mexican fear that his flag of truce would not be respected?

Or was there another and more serious cause for his perturbation?

On the face of it, almost everything was in the attackers' favor. They had a vast numerical superiority, and although they could not avoid a certain amount of losses, careful management could restrict these to the younger and more headstrong Hopi braves who would be all too eager to lead the assault. So once Méndez-Castillo had rejoined his companions, there would be only minimal danger. Only something completely unexpected and untoward could turn the scales in the Texians' favor under the circumstances.

Yet Ole Devil grew ever more convinced that the major believed—or was afraid—something might go wrong.

The young Texian wished that he could take his eyes from Méndez-Castillo and find out if anything was happening on the rim. However, he knew that his companions were watching and would warn him immediately if there was any sign of the enemy's setting its mounts into motion.

Even as Ole Devil was reaching that point in his conclusions, he felt as if he had been touched by an icy hand. A thought, alarming in its portent, drove into him. It was one, he told himself bitterly, that should have occurred to him right away. In exculpation, despite his having slept soundly and woken considerably refreshed, there had been so many other things demanding his attention that he might be excused for having failed to take such a contingency into consideration.

Except that the lapse might cost the defenders their lives more quickly than would otherwise have been the case!

While the steeply sloping ground on the downstream side of the U-shaped basin would be impassable, at least with any speed, on horseback, men could walk—or even run—over its uneven surface without too much difficulty. Certainly they would have a better chance of approaching unseen than riders. Especially when the attention of their proposed victims was being diverted and held in another direction.

"Very well!" Méndez-Castillo said, disturbed by the satanic-faced Texian's unremitting scrutiny—which was beginning to induce a sensation of religious-inspired superstitious dread—and wanting to remove himself from it. Starting to rein his horse around, he spoke louder than was necessary. "Colonel Villena is not an unreasonable or impatient man. He will give you an hour in which to consider his proposal and make up your minds. But I must warn you, if at the end of that time you still persist in this foolish and futile defiance, we will strike you down without mercy."

"My thanks to Colonel Villena for his consideration," Ole Devil replied, addressing the words to the Mexican officer's back as he had completed the turning of his mount and started it moving while speaking. "And tell him that we apologize to the widows of the brave men he will be sending to their deaths."

*   *   *

"The stupid fool!" the commanding officer of Company Five spit out, as he sat his horse with the other senior Mexicans on the rim and watched Major Méndez-Castillo bringing the parley to an end. "He hasn't kept them talking nearly long enough!"

While the words echoed Villena's sentiments, the fact that they had been uttered by his greatest rival made him stiffen and glare around.

"I didn't notice you showing any willingness to volunteer for the task, *Major* Santoval!" the self-appointed colonel snorted back.

Santoval could not have disputed the comment, even if he had wished to do so. Although approving—even if only silently and to himself—of his superior's strategy, he had been all too aware of the danger involved in carrying out a most important aspect of it. So he had studiously refused to meet

Villena's eyes or respond in any other way to the call for a volunteer to take on the precarious assignment.

From the scout's description of the Texians' defensive positions and their surroundings, Villena had concluded that attaining his desire for revenge would be anything but a sure thing. He was all too aware that success, or failure, hinged entirely upon the Hopis' willingness to fight. They had not been sufficiently exposed to the influences of Christianity to have discarded their belief in the primitive superstitions of their nation. So, because they remembered that the previous failure had been in a similar location at Santa Cristóbal Bay, meeting a determined resistance at this site could cause them to assume that their war medicine was bad. Once that happened, they would lose heart and be grudging of their lives to such an extent that they were unlikely to press home an attack.

With that in mind, the "colonel" had decided to employ trickery. It was his intention, he had explained to his subordinates, to have two companies move on foot down the steeply sloping ground over which it would be impossible for them to ride horses at speed. To prevent the impromptu infantry from being discovered prematurely, he would cause the defenders to be distracted by sending an officer under a flag of truce ostensibly to deliver terms for a surrender.

The first snag to Villena's plan had been persuading one of his majors, whose rank made them the obvious choice, to perform the vitally important part in the proceedings. In all fairness, Santoval had not been alone in evading the duty. Like him, all but Méndez-Castillo had excused themselves on the ground that they could not speak sufficient English to conduct negotiations. Their obvious reluctance had infected and brought an equal lack of cooperation from their juniors. Nor had the attempts of the "colonel" at minimizing the risks produced the desired results. While they had been willing to concede that the leader of the Texians might be a caballero close to their own social standing and, as such, imbued with the well-born Anglo-Saxon's respect for a flag of truce, the same could not be said of the men who would be with him.

Fear of the consequences, rather than any moral objections to the betrayal of the rules governing the conducting of a formally requested parley, had been responsible for the majors' reluctance to come forward. Their easy consciences had dismissed the latter as excusable on the ground that they were dealing with rebels and not fighting an enemy. From their limited acquaintance and what they had been told, they considered the majority of Texians complete barbarians with small regard for civilized conventions and less where the sanctity of human life was concerned. Even if such men could be trusted to remain passive while their superior was talking, they would open fire upon whoever was conducting the parley if the foot party should be seen approaching before he had withdrawn. What was more, if the plot succeeded, before they were wiped out, the defenders would make him a prime target in revenge for his betrayal.

It had only been when dark with barely controlled anger, the "colonel" had hinted at dire consequences in the future if the plan fell through and they were compelled to retire empty-handed that Méndez-Castillo had reluctantly offered his services. Of all the officers present, he was the least able to refuse. Not only was he fluent in English, but his formerly wealthy family had suffered serious business reverses and was to a great extent dependent upon the charity of Villena's father. So he had volunteered with what grace he could muster.

Although Méndez-Castillo's bearing and attitude had not been calculated to induce wild optimism among his fellow officers, he had appeared to be carrying out his duty in a satisfactory fashion. For the plan to succeed, he had to hold the Texians' attention. At first, despite his somewhat nervous manner, it had seemed that he would do so. The gringo enlisted men had remained in their shallow rifle pits, which formed a half circle around the tarpaulin-covered mound of ammunition boxes, but they had watched him instead of

their fronts. Major Piña and Gómez had already started their
respective companies advancing on foot, but they were still
far from an advantageous distance when Méndez-Castillo
terminated the parley by turning away.

Cold rage boiled through Villena. Because of the Hopi
braves' growing disenchantment with the pursuit through
terrain so vastly different from that in which they had
been born and raised, he had been compelled to let their
chiefs tell them of his "medicine" for ensuring victory. The
strength of his authority had been further weakened among
them by the realization that much of the valuable loot they
were anticipating had gone over the river and would require
a further chase. If it was seen that his present scheme was
not going according to plan, they might refuse to fight and
certainly would not give of their best if they did.

There was, the "colonel" concluded, only one thing to do.

"Charge!" Villena thundered, sending his restlessly moving horse bounding forward.

Realizing the danger of any further delay, the rest of the
Mexicans repeated the order and followed their superior.
Letting out their war whoops, the Hopis obeyed, and the
mass of riders began to swoop down toward the small band
of Texians, who must stand and fight as they had no means of
doing anything else.

16

GOOD OLD *YELLOW STONE*

"Watch that slope!" Ole Devil Hardin shouted, following the advice himself as he noticed Major Ramón Méndez-Castillo throw a quick look in that direction and then encourage the horse to move faster.

Only the briefest inspection was needed to inform the young Texian that his conclusion had been correct. However, he could also take some small comfort from the realization that the enemy's treacherous plot had gone amiss because of the major's premature departure. While a number of Hopis and their Mexican officers were approaching on foot, making the most of what little cover was available, they were still much too far away to pose the threat they would have been if the trick had not miscarried.

Startled exclamations told Ole Devil that his instructions had been carried out by the men in the rifle pits closest to the sloping ground. However, they all were experienced fighters and did not waste powder and shot by opening fire at such a long range.

Listening to Ole Devil's warning, Méndez-Castillo knew that his superior's ploy had failed. His glance had shown him that Companies Four and Nine were still much too far away to play their part. Even as he was returning his gaze to the front, he heard "Colonel" Abrahán Felipe Gonzáles de Villena y Danvila's word of command and saw the remaining companies of the Arizona Hopi Activos Regiment commence the attack. So he applied his spurs to his mount's flanks, causing it to increase its pace, in the hope of avoiding the wrath which he felt sure the defenders would direct upon him in repayment for his treachery.

The Hopi brave carrying the white flag had also started to turn away from the Texians. At the sight of his companions beginning to advance, he saw a way of gaining a great honor. It was a dangerous—some might even consider foolhardy—thing to do, but he had elected to arm himself with a lance and there were obligations in accepting such a distinction.[1] One was an utter disregard for personal safety in battle.

Reversing his mount's direction with a speed and precision which would not have shamed the finest polo player and pony, the brave dropped the head of his weapon forward. Without even trying to shake off the white shirt which had served as a flag, he gave his "kill or die" cry and signaled his intentions with his heels. Instantly the well-trained horse sprang forward. There was no need for him to think of selecting a victim. He had already decided that only one was suitable and would bring the acclaim deserved by his deed.

The gringo with the face of *el diablo*!

Aiming the lance's needle-sharp head at the center of the chest of the tall, slim Texian, the brave guided the horse toward him.

Although Ole Devil was looking away, he heard the Hopi's yell and the sound of the horse approaching. Knowing something of the Indians' regard for the lance as a weapon, he guessed what was happening and that he might have been chosen as the victim. What was more, because he had not

1. Further details of the importance set by Indian warriors to carrying a war lance are given in *Sidewinder*.

laid aside his pistols while conducting the parley, he had the means to defend himself.

Swinging his attention to the front and confirming his suspicions, Ole Devil was already lifting his right-hand pistol. However, he was not the only member of his party who had appreciated the danger. Equally aware of the responsibilities which went with carrying a lance, although he could not be sure that the house Indian Hopis—with whom he had had no prior contact—adhered to such precepts, Tom Wolf had been keeping the warrior under observation. At the first suggestion of trouble, the Tejas chief snapped his rifle upward.

Even as Ole Devil was squeezing the Manton's trigger, he heard the crack of two rifle shots, but too late for him to prevent himself from firing. Hit between the eyes and in the chest, either of which wounds would have been sufficient to kill him, the brave was flung bodily backward from his horse. The lance flew from his hand as he went down, and frightened by the weapons going off in front of it, his mount swerved aside. At the same moment that death took the Hopi, the bullet fired by old Jube struck the back of Méndez-Castillo's skull. Killed instantly, the Mexican joined his companion in crashing to the ground and became their regiment's first two casualties.

Although Ole Devil saw his party had scored first blood in the encounter, he knew it was small cause for congratulations. Nor would it have the slightest effect upon the inevitable ending.

Well over two hundred mounted attackers were pouring into the basin and rushing closer at an ever-increasing rate as they urged their horses to gallop!

Nearly a hundred more assailants, seeing that there was no hope of drawing nearer undetected, gave vent to war yells and started to run forward!

Following his orders, Sergeant Smith moved back until he joined Sammy Cope, who was behind the tarpaulin-covered mound of ammunition. Taking out and cocking his pistol, the noncom knelt and placed its muzzle on the tip of the quick match cord. The destruction of the supplies was his duty, which would fall to Cope if he should be prevented from carrying it out for some reason.

Scanning the enemy's ranks as he tossed the empty pistol behind him and onto the mound, so that it would not be taken away after the battle, Ole Devil noticed how the older Mexicans and Hopi war leaders were allowing their more imprudent juniors and the younger braves to draw ahead. The same thing had happened at Santa Cristóbal Bay, so he was not surprised to find out who would be bearing the brunt of his men's fire.

Despite being little older than his subalterns, Villena was one of those who were showing caution. He had done so during the previous battle, and it had saved his life. Trying to locate him among the swarming mass of riders, Ole Devil intended to prevent him from escaping a second time if an opportunity was presented.

Onward thundered the attackers!

Already the defenders were opening fire upon the still closely packed horde!

By Ole Devil's side, Tommy Okasi drew and loosed a *yanagi-ha* arrow, extracting another from his quiver with deft speed as soon as it was on its way. Dropping the rifle with which he had justified Méndez-Castillo's fears of how the treacherous betrayal of the flag of truce would be replayed, Jube snatched up his second weapon and put it to equally good use. Others aimed, fired, and exchanged their spent caplocks for the loaded reserve arms laid close at hand.

At each shot, a man or a horse went down, but the remainder continued to charge without hesitation or alarm over the losses.

Another hundred yards and the leading Hopis would be on the defenders!

Seventy-five!

Every Texian and Tejas Indian had used three of his weapons to good effect!

Then it happened!

Louder than the barking of the defenders' rifles, even making itself heard above the rumbling thunder from the horses' hooves, came an unexpected noise.

"Whoo-ooo-whoo!"

The eerie sound, magnified and echoing from the sheer walls of the gorge, caused all the Hopis in particular to stare in that direction and brought the dismounted braves to a halt. It was something beyond their comprehension. So was the sight that greeted their amazed gazes a moment later.

"Good old *Yellow Stone!*" Ole Devil breathed, without looking around. "Let's hope those horses aren't like Di's mules!"

Coming from where it had been concealed up to then by the sides of the gorge was the thing which had caused the young Texian to be concerned over traveling along the banks of the Brazos River with the mule train. He had known that having been brought in sections from the United States and assembled on arrival, a steamboat operated between the coast and the inland cities. However, Diamond Hitch Brindley had assured him that her animals had had sufficient contact with the *Yellow Stone* and similar vessels which plied the Red River in Arkansas to have lost all fear of them.

The same did not apply to the Hopis—or their mounts!

In spite of being smaller than the great passenger and cargo carriers using the mighty Mississippi–Missouri river system, the *Yellow Stone* was still an impressive sight as she emerged from the gorge. Smoke, flames, and sparks—the latter created deliberately on her captain's orders to enhance the dramatic effect—belched from her tall stack, and her wheels churned the water as they drove her along. A trio of four-pounder boat cannon had been fitted at her bows since the commencement of hostility, and these were manned, ready for use.

Coming from Arizona, the Indians had never seen a boat larger than was needed for an oxen-powered or compass type of ferry or even one that was driven by a sail. Nor were they aware of such a device as a steam engine as a means of

motive power. So the sight of the *Yellow Stone* bearing down
on them was the cause of consternation and terror. None of
them could imagine what the strange apparition might be.

Turning his vessel toward the western shore, with all the
easy facility granted by the paddle wheels on each side, the
captain tugged on the lanyard, and the whistle emitted another of its steam-powered whoops. In echo to the sound,
the three cannon bellowed and vomited forth their loads of
canister.[2]

Great as the shock delivered to the Hopis by the *Yellow
Stone*'s appearance might be, it had an even more adverse
effect upon their horses. Before the tempest of balls from
the cannon reached them, the animals were registering their
alarm by rearing, plunging, or swerving wildly in an attempt
to get away from the terrible fire-breathing monstrosity that
was coming toward them.

Nor did the Hopis and Mexicans who had avoided being
unseated try to regain control of their panic-stricken mounts
and resume the attack. Instead, like the animals, the braves
in particular had only one idea: to flee as swiftly as possible
from the demoniac device which they believed had been
summoned up by some magical power of the gringo with the
face of *el diablo*, the devil.

In an instant, the charge that had threatened to overrun
the Texians' positions had been reduced to chaos. With one
exception, even the Mexicans—who knew what the *Yellow
Stone* was—did nothing to avert the panic. Instead, they
joined in the flight. Nor was the exception, Villena, able to
prevent the mass departure.

Thrown from his horse as it took grave exception to the
appearance of the steamboat, the "colonel" had contrived to
alight without injury. However, his pistol had flown from his
grasp while he was falling. Leaping to his feet and snatching

2. Canister: a number of small balls that were packed in a metallic cylinder for ease of loading, but that spread like the charge from a shotgun on
being fired.

the *épée-de-combat* from its sheath, he tried to avert the rout. Not one of the men who were still mounted took the slightest notice of his yells. Instead, they scattered and fled in the direction from which they had come. If he had looked, he would have learned that the two companies on the sloping ground were also in full flight.

Finding themselves left on foot and with no means of flight gave the Hopis the courage of desperation. Screaming war cries that held a timbre of terror, they rushed at the men in the rifle pits with the intention of dying fighting.

Rage filled Villena as he realized that he had been abandoned by the majority of his regiment. Glaring around furiously, he located the man who had brought about his downfall and saw his chance of taking revenge. As he looked, the young Texian—whose face appeared even more like that of the devil than ever—shot a charging brave. Doing so had emptied his pistol, and he did not have another on his person.

Realizing what it meant, the "colonel" spit out a delighted exclamation and dashed forward. If he had been in control of his emotions, he would never have attempted such a wild attack. In his present frame of mind, he thought only of impaling on the *épée-de-combat* the man for whom he had developed an all-consuming hatred.

On discharging the shot from his second pistol, Ole Devil released it. His right hand flashed across to close around the concave ivory hilt of the bowie knife. Even as he was drawing it from its sheath, he became aware of another threat to his life. Face distorted with rage, Villena was almost upon him.

Seeming to act of its own volition, the bowie knife swung to the right. The great blade met the advancing *épée-de-combat* and swept it aside. There was a major difference between the two weapons. Where the sword was designed purely for thrusting with its point, the shape of the knife's blade gave it a far greater scope. The rounded back of the blade was excellent for parrying without endangering the cutting edge, but the latter or the equally sharp false edge could be used to slash and thrust.

Disengaging his weapon as soon as it had deflected Villena's blade away from him, Ole Devil performed a lightning-fast backhand chop. The false edge made contact before the Mexican could think of retaliation or evasion, passing under his chin to lay open his throat. As the weapon came free, although his every instinct told him he had already delivered a mortal blow, the Texian could not resist striking again. Around lashed his hand, directing the cutting edge to just below Villena's right ear. Biting in until it met bone, the blade shoved its recipient aside. His weight dragged him free, and he blundered on for a few involuntary steps until he collapsed facedown across the mound of ammunition that had, in part, cost him his life.

Then it was over.

Lowering his bloodstained knife, Ole Devil looked around. Not a single living enemy remained in the basin. Apart from a couple of minor wounds, the defenders had come through the fighting unscathed. Giving a sigh of relief, he walked to meet the men who were coming off the *Yellow Stone* and wondered how they had managed to arrive so fortunately.[3]

Di Brindley was galloping toward the opposite bank, waving her hat and yelling in delight. Returning her salutation, Ole Devil felt sure that the consignment of caplocks and ammunition was safe. With the help of her mule train, he could complete the delivery and give Major General Samuel Houston a powerful aid in the struggle to gain independence for Texas.

3. Having met with Mannen Blaze's party while on a routine patrol, the captain of the *Yellow Stone* had agreed to go in search of the mule train. He had been contacted by the Tejas scout whom Ole Devil had sent to find him and, learning of the danger, had come prepared to deal with it. Guessing that the Hopis would never have seen a steamboat, he had added to its shock value by blowing the whistle and causing the flames, extra-thick smoke, and sparks to be given out.